The
Time
Walker

Geoff Moran

Published independently in 2025

Text © Geoff Moran 2025

A catalogue record for this
book is available from the
National Library of Australia

This book is available in the print and Kindle formats.

Dedicated to my youngest sister

Diane Joy Eriksson nee Moran

who passed away 21st May 2020.

Never forgotten.

R.I.P.

Table of Contents

Chapter 1

FIRST POLICE CONTACT

It was early morning, about 9:30 a.m., when the young man walked into the police station. The female constable ran her eyes over him while she was attending an old gentleman who had had his dog stolen.

The young man was dressed in jeans, Doc Marten boots, and a hoodie. Nothing unusual about him, but he had his hood up and was wearing a baseball cap over that and was also wearing a pair of sunglasses even though he had just come in from the street. The constable's senses were on full alert, especially as he had one hand in the pocket of his jacket. The old man was rambling on, and she was only listening to him with ten percent of her attention, especially as the young man started taking his hand out of his pocket. She relaxed when she saw that he was holding an envelope; however, he was wearing gloves, and the day was not cold enough to warrant gloves. The youth leaned towards her and dropped the envelope on the counter. He only spoke one word: "CAPTAIN." Then he turned and walked out of the station and down the footpath.

She left the envelope where it had fallen and finished up with the elderly gentleman as quickly as she politely could.

She reached into the pocket of her tunic and removed a pair of gloves and put them on. That way, she would not get in contact with any poison on the envelope or wipe out any fingerprints. She pressed a hidden bell push, and when her companion arrived, she said, "Watch the counter for me for a while."

The envelope was swiftly taken into the detective section of the station when she spoke to the detective in charge.

"Just had a strange experience, Captain."

"What's that, constable?"

"Just had this envelope delivered by a young fella, and he only said one word: 'CAPTAIN.'"

The captain donned a pair of gloves and lifted the envelope, giving it a light squeeze.

"Feels like a memory stick. Give me that letter opener, and we will check out what's inside."

The envelope was carefully slit along the top edge, and the captain turned the envelope over. A memory stick dropped out onto the desk.

"Where is the IT person? I want to see what's on the memory stick, but don't want to bring any virus into our system."

The IT person was there in seconds.

"Yeah, captain, what can I do for you?"

"Put on a pair of gloves and check out this stick and make sure that there are no viruses on it before I open it up on my computer."

"Okay, just give me a moment."

Within minutes, the memory stick was back with the captain. "All clear, Captain." The captain plugged it in, and he and the constable waited while the computer opened the file.

"Bloody old computers they send us from head office. Man could make a cup of coffee while it opens."

"Right, here it is."

"Video of street scene. Looks like downtown, but years ago, in the middle of the night. Who is this woman walking along the street?"

By this time, the comments had attracted a couple more detectives who were always curious. A young, attractive female teenager was walking along by herself when a Mazda bongo van pulled up alongside, and the driver spoke to the girl. Slowly, the side door in the van opened, and a man stepped out and whipped a hand over her mouth and dragged her into the van. The sliding door was slammed shut, and the bongo van drove off. The camera scene swept down to take in the number plate of the van. The movie came to an end. The detectives all were silent, as was the constable. The captain was the first to speak.

"Right, what you all just saw is confidential and is not to go outside this room. Now, did anyone else write down the number plate?"

There were a number of nods.

"Check that we all have the same number."

The numbers written down were all the same.

"Constable, go and get the video from the CCTV for the front desk. I want to have a look at this young man. Detectives, find out who owns or owned that bongo van, and I want the information as soon as possible."

The whole room moved as one, with people heading for computers and telephones.

It was not long before information started coming back to the captain.

"Not much we can tell from the CCTV camera in the foyer."

"Right, two of you head off and have a look along the street and see if this young bloke shows up on any of the CCTV units on the shops. I want this guy. Anyone who turns up and gives us a video of an abduction is top of my list to talk to. Constable, get some copies made of our CCTV image of him and get them down to the traffic boys. They might see him walking the street or get him driving a car."

"Captain, got some information on the bongo van. Stolen and found burnt out. Got the name and address of the owner at the time, too. Now listen to this. This is the strange bit. It happened twenty-five years ago."

"What! You're telling me this young bloke has come in and dropped a video on the counter that was shot twenty-five years ago? He wasn't even born then, so where has the video been for all those years?"

"Captain, that's the information from the transport department in Sydney."

"Something strange here about the whole situation. Let's be patient till the guys report back on any luck they have finding this young fellow."

An hour later, everyone was back in the detective's room. The captain spoke to all of them.

"Well, people, did we have any luck finding the young bloke?"

Just heads shaking no.

"Right, the IT guy has got a better computer setup, so we can all have another look at the video." There was a shuffling of chairs as everyone found a seat in front of a bigger screen. The IT person spoke first.

"When I start this video, I want you all to see how the sides of the images seem to curve around the main focused image on the screen. I have not seen that before. Right, here we go."

The video started playing while everyone stared intently at the screen. The video came to an end.

"Play it again."

The video was played about five times before the captain spoke again.

"Right, thoughts, people?"

The constable spoke first.

"Fashion on the girl is what was in fashion 25 years ago."

"Does anybody recognize the street scene?"

Again, silence.

"All right, what missing persons in the state do we have for that time line?"

A detective spoke up. "Two young women, within a couple of months of each other. Disappeared coming home from a night out. Walking alone and never seen again. Large police search in both towns but very little evidence to go on."

"Right, give me the names and towns, and I will take this information further up the line of command. Keep this information in this room. I don't want the press getting hold of it and turning it into some sort of mystery."

"Right, back to work."

The station moved back into its normal mode, and other issues took over the thoughts of everyone, but the captain.

His thoughts went back 25 years to when he was a young constable, and he worked on one of these cases here in town. Not a week went by that he did not have a moment when he thought about that disappearance.

"I.T."

"Yes, boss?"

"Make me up some still copies of the background out of that video, please."

"Will do. Give me an hour or so."

Chapter 2

REVISIT THE PAST

An hour later, the captain had a bunch of photos in his hand. He walked through to the desk constable. "Constable, get somebody to take over the front desk, get a vehicle, and pick me up out front."

"Yes, sir."

A few minutes later, the constable pulled up out front of the police station, and the captain climbed into the front passenger seat.

"Right turn first and take us into the town centre, constable."

"Where are we going, sir?"

"You'll have all revealed in 5 minutes, so be patient. Turn here and drive up this road a bit. Now pull into the shade of that big tree and park there. Park parallel to the road. Now turn off the engine."

The captain shuffled the photos and selected one. "Twenty-five years ago, these trees were tiny, just like in this photo. Have a look, and can you see the front of the shops still?"

"Looks very similar, captain."

"Right, let's get out and see if we can find any more similar images."

The captain handed over some more photos, and the pair slowly walked up the street, picking out features in the background of the photos.

"Captain, if this is not the location in these photos, then it is very close to it."

"Well, it is nice to know that I am not going insane, constable. This was a terrible case with no evidence, family accused of the abduction, friends pitted against friends over the whole affair."

"What do we do now, captain?"

"Find that young fellow. He is the answer to all our questions. Why would you drop off the video and just walk away?"

"Twenty-five years and nothing, and now this. Let's find the owners of the bongo van and see if the stolen story was the truth or not. Back to the station and let the boys loose. I want the real truth to come out at last."

Ten minutes later, they were back in the police station.

The captain called a quick meeting.

"Right, people, the constable and I are almost 100 percent sure that this video was shot here in town. The little trees in the video are now grown 15 to 20 meters along the footpath, but there are enough shops from that era still there to confirm our thinking. Twenty-five years ago, I was a young constable, fresh out of the academy, and I remember this case clear as a bell, and I want to close it off this time. Find the owners of the bongo van. Find the young fellow, and no talking to anyone about this or we will have a press circus in town. Any thoughts, any information, bring them to me immediately."

The captain went to his office to call headquarters and bring them up to speed on what had happened. Total disbelief was the first reaction at headquarters, but the truth finally sank in, and it was agreed that two senior detectives would come up from Sydney to help out.

Everyone was working on doing what the captain asked for until well after knock-off time.

"Right, everyone go home and get some shut-eye and come to work tomorrow refreshed. On your way."

The office soon emptied except for the captain, who had a final look at the video. Then he too called it a day.

Chapter 3

MEETING THE MAYOR

9 a.m. the next morning, the office was full, and everyone was talking at once when the captain walked in with two strange faces.

"People, I want to introduce the two detectives from headquarters. Detectives Brown and Kanowski. They are here to work with us, so share any information, because the only way we will solve this is to be a team. All right?"

Heads nodded in agreement, and everyone started to review the information gathered from the day before and looked at what had come in overnight regarding the bongo van.

"Well, captain, we have an address for the owner of the bongo van."

"Right, let's just sit on that information for the time being until we know where we are going. Constable, take our two new friends up to where you and I were parked yesterday and go through the photos with them, but after they have had a look at the video. I have a meeting with the mayor, who wants to know what we were doing yesterday walking along the street looking at photos. I swear that guy has more spies than ASIO."

People moved out to get their respective duties done while the captain closed his office and headed off to the café that the mayor had nominated for their impromptu meeting.

The mayor was already waiting when the captain arrived. The mayor stood up and shook hands.

"Hello, captain. What news do you have for me? By the way, while I was waiting here for you, this envelope was delivered to me to give to you. I hope I am not becoming your postman."

The captain's heart started beating faster. "Who delivered this to you, and when, Mr. Mayor?"

"Well, about 10 minutes ago. A young fellow. You know how they dress. Hoodie, boots, jeans."

"Where did he go, Mayor?"

"Well, he just dropped it off on the table and said 'CAPTAIN' and turned and left. I thought it was a bit strange that he knew you were coming."

"I have to go, Mr. Mayor. This is very important to me."

The captain turned and almost ran from the café back to the police station.

He was calling for the IT person before he even stopped walking.

"Check this out for me. I can tell it is another message from our young friend."

By this time, anyone who was in the room was waiting for the IT person to bring the memory stick back to the captain.

"All clean, captain. No virus."

"Right, play it on the big screen and let's see what we have this time."

The computer opened the video, and everyone held their breaths as the bongo van came into the image. There were trees and large rocks all around. The camera zoomed in on the number plate, then backed out to show the sliding door on the van opening.

The driver came around and started pulling a large sack from the van. The second person climbed out to help. Their faces were hidden by baseball caps and turned-up collars of their jackets. They both looked around, and then they took an end each and walked away into the bush. After maybe 50 meters, they came to a hole dug in the ground, and with a combined effort, they threw the sack into the ground. There was something weighty in the sack.

They both walked back to the bongo van, and a couple of minutes later, came back with shovels and started to fill in the hole.

The video came to an end.

The room was silent.

The captain spoke first.

"Get up to the café on the corner and see if they have CCTV. The rest of you spread out along the street and look for cameras. I want this young bloke here in the station. How did he get a video of something that happened twenty-five years ago in the bush? IT, check out this video and tell me is it real or fake, and why are the faces of the men hidden?"

People started moving out of the squad room in a rush.

The chief, with the two detectives from headquarters, went into the chief's office.

They all sat down, and the chief ran his hands over his face and back over his head. "How is this guy doing this? He is driving me around the twist. I barely got any sleep last night, now he is playing with us again today."

The two detectives looked at each other with questioning looks on their faces.

Just then, the captain's phone rang. He took it out of his pocket and looked at the screen.

"No number." He answered it after clicking the loudspeaker on.

"Chief Inspector Wilson, good morning."

"Hello, captain. Still looking for me, I see."

"Who are you, and how did you get these videos, young fellow?"

"Captain, I can't tell you everything. You have to do some work."

"Why are you calling now if you won't help me out?"

"Captain, there is a reward offered for information, and that's what I have given you. Have you got the money there in the police station?"

"No, it doesn't work like that. All we have is a video of an abduction and another showing two men throwing something into a hole in the ground. That's not going to get any conviction, and we don't know where the hole in the ground even is."

"Come on, captain. Do I have to do everything for you? Look at the video again and where the hole is in the video. When you have found the remains, I will give you all the information you will need for a conviction. Bye for now, captain."

He hung up.

"Let's look at the second video again and see what he was talking about."

The three went back out to the large computer and ran the video again. The three looked blankly at it, then ran it again and again, still not seeing anything.

"Constable, come in here and have a look at this video. Your young eyes might see what us old fogies are missing."

The constable came in from the front counter and sat down. The video started playing, and immediately she said, "Stop it there." The screen froze. "Captain, look up there in the background. See the rocks? I have seen those rocks before somewhere, but I am not sure where."

"Constable, find somebody from the local bushwalking club and have the traffic boys pick them up and bring them here."

"Yes, sir."

The three detectives sat studying the video for the next 30 minutes until they thought their eyes were going to fall out of their heads.

The rest of the squad room slowly came back into the office, and with negative results regarding any info on their informant.

It was an hour later that the constable escorted in a fit-looking gentleman about 40 years of age.

"Captain, this is Mr. Connor, who is the president of the local bushwalking club."

"Good morning, Mr. Connor. Thank you for your assistance in this matter. I want to show you a video, and I need you to see if you recognize where it was shot by the background in the video."

"I will do my best, captain, but no guarantees."

"I understand, but please try."

The captain started the video, and the bushwalker immediately said, "Stop there."

"Those rocks in the background are in the national park near Watson Waterfall. Unusual vertical striations in the basalt. I would recognize it anywhere."

"Right, thank you, Mr. Connor. Now we need to impose on you even more. Please go with our forensic team and show them exactly where you reckon the video is showing these rocks."

"Constable, get some still shots, and you go with the team and Mr. Connor and call me when you find the location. I want to be there at that time. Thank you, Mr. Connor."

Fifteen minutes later, the constable and a forensic team trooped out and climbed into cars, and under the direction of Mr. Connor, headed out to Watson Waterfall.

"Is this guy just shooting videos to have the police running here and there, or is he trying some sort of scam so he gets some reward money? He is driving me around the bend with these videos."

"Hang in there, captain.

Chapter 4

FIRST BODY

It was 1 p.m. when they got a radio call from the forensic team.

"What have you got, guys?"

"Better come out, Captain, as there is something there in the ground for sure."

"Right, wait till I get there before starting to dig." He called the detectives from head office to come with him.

There was no mucking about as the captain had the lights and siren on all the way to the national park.

He pulled the car up, and they all got out. "The constable was there waiting for him."

"This way, gentlemen."

They made their way through some low branches until they arrived at the area nominated by the forensic people.

"This is the area, Captain."

"Well, let's get started digging. We don't have all day."

Two young, fit officers in overalls started digging where the forensic team had marked out a rectangle on the ground. The soil was soft from recent rains, and they made good progress until one of the shovels hit a metallic object.

The digging stopped as one of the forensic guys had a dig with a hand shovel and came up with a couple of old beer cans, which were put to one side.

"Well, that confirms somebody dug and backfilled a hole here," said the captain. The young men started digging again and soon came upon a plastic sheet spread across the hole.

The forensic people took over the excavation work, slowly scraping the soil from on top of the plastic sheet. Soon the whole of the excavation was exposed, and the plastic sheet was carefully taken off and bagged as evidence. Even after all this time, a match to a roll could be found in a shed somewhere. Underneath were the remains of a hemp bag, and gentle scraping exposed the bones of a hand.

The head of the forensic team spoke for the first time. "Well, Captain, your informant was correct. We have the remains of a cadaver here, so from now on, this is a crime scene. I would ask everyone not in my team to please leave the area. I will get any information to you as soon as possible. Could the constable please stay on here as a driver and assistant for us, please?"

"Constable, stay and assist as much as you can."

"Yes, Captain."

"Right, everyone else, back to the station for a round-table meeting."

Everyone not in the forensic team headed back to their cars.

Back in the office at the police station, everyone headed for the coffee machine, then found a seat at the conference table.

"Right, IT, I want you to see if you can trace the phone number of the young fellow who rang me earlier."

"Captain, I have already tried, and I have been working with the Telstra experts while you have been out of the office. This young bloke is very smart. When he rang you, his call used hundreds of phones around Australia. His call kept jumping from phone to phone that was not being used at the time. Telstra had never seen anything like it and could not help in any way at getting his number."

"So, we have come up against another dead end. Well, it appears that we have the remains of a victim out in the national park. We have a video of her being abducted and the number plate of a burnt-out Bongo van. We have a video of two men burying what could be the victim, but we can't see their faces. So, we don't have anything to go on at this time."

Just at that moment, the captain's phone rang.

Upon taking it out of his pocket, he looked at the screen, and it said, blocked number. "Well, let's see who it is." He answered the phone. "Good afternoon, Captain Wilson speaking. How may I help?"

"Hello, Captain, this is your friendly young fellow that you want so badly calling."

The captain mouthed, "It's him."

"Captain, don't put it on loudspeaker and don't try and lie to me, as I will know immediately and will hang up. Do you understand?"

"Yes, no loudspeaker."

"Good, now we go on to the next step. Time for you to get your superiors to start getting the reward ready to transfer to my account.

Now don't give me any crap about not being able to do this. When you have the money ready, I will give you the faces of the abductors, plus a lot, lot more. Now, you will want a search warrant, but before you go to get that, I want the name of the magistrate who will issue it to you. Is that understood, Captain?"

"Yes, I understand, but what difference does it make which magistrate we go to for a search warrant?"

"Captain, have you ever thought that twenty-five years ago the killers were young people and now could be respected members of the community?"

"Are you telling me that the killers are professional people?" This was said with a note of incredulity by the captain.

"You just do like I ask, Captain, and you and I will get along just fine."

The phone went dead.

Everyone started speaking at once. The captain held up both hands. "Quiet, please. The young bloke has said no more speaker phones, or he will disappear. He wants the government to start getting the ball rolling for the reward that is offered. When the money is ready, he will give us a lot more information on where we need to search and the facial views of the two abductors. I want everyone to finish what you are doing and go back to what you were doing before all this started. I need not remind you young people to keep all this quiet, or we might frighten the young bloke and the killers away. You two detectives from Sydney, come into my office, and we will have a talk about the reward."

With that said, the captain stood up and went to his office, followed by the two Sydney detectives.

"Shut the door and take a seat, guys. The other thing he mentioned, but which I didn't want to say too much in front of the team, is who we will approach for a search warrant. He inferred that some of the legal profession might be involved with what happened twenty-five years ago. How he will check them out is beyond me, but he is so far ahead of us that I have to go with what he says; otherwise, all information will stop."

"Bloody hell," said one of the detectives.

"Guys, I want you to go back to Sydney and speak to the big boss and explain what is happening here and that I am not some mentally deranged copper from the bush. Keep the number of people you speak to a minimum. If this gets out, the 5th estate and the TV people will turn this into the biggest circus you have ever seen. Bad enough that my people have been involved, but it now looks like he only wants to deal with me."

"I have wished for twenty-five years to be able to solve this case, but I never thought that it would be like this. Do you have any questions or anything to help me out?"

Neither detective spoke, but both shook their heads.

"Thanks, guys, for coming up here. Call me when you get to Sydney. Please keep all this to yourselves."

The two Sydney detectives left the captain's office and headed out to their car.

The captain headed into his office and closed the door. He hung his head in his hands and sighed deeply. Never before in his working life had he had anything like this happen to him, and he had never heard of anything like this happening anywhere else either.

He didn't know what to do now.

Chapter 5

THE DISCLOSURE

It was late afternoon when he got a phone call from the forensic team leader.

"Captain?"

"Yes, go ahead."

"Well, we have removed all the remains, and we will head off back to the lab in Sydney. We have run a lot of police tape around the grave site, but to be honest, I would not expect to find anything else there. The remains are of a young female. The damage to the leg and arm bones shows she was badly beaten, but this is off the cuff at the moment. I will have more in a couple of days."

"OK. Give me a call when you know more, and thanks for your help."

The captain hung up and put the phone in his pocket.

He was feeling very despondent and was feeling very alone with a lot of weight on his shoulders.

It was just on knock-off time when there was a knock on his door.

"Come in."

The constable who was the start point for the whole investigation came into the office.

"Close the door, constable, and tell me what went on out there today."

"Well, sir, they exhumed the skeleton of a female, about 18 to 20 years old, the forensic people said. They have taken all the remains with them back to Sydney. We have wrapped the whole area in police tape but left the grave open at this time."

"You have done a great job, constable, and I will not forget what you have done. I believe this will be the remains of a missing girl from twenty-five years ago. The abduction nearly tore this town apart with families blaming each other and friends. It was a terrible time. I just hope they can get some DNA from the remains so the family can have closure. It is hard on families that never know what has happened to their loved ones. Go and get a car and take me home. I have had enough for one day."

Ten minutes later, the chief was dropped off at his house. He walked in and went to the refrigerator and grabbed a cold beer. His wife said, "Go and sit out in the pergola, and I will bring you some nibblies. Wind down and try not to think too much about what has happened."

The captain nodded and headed out into the cool of the pergola with its grapevines growing across the roof.

He settled down and sipped his beer, at which time his phone rang.

"Bloody hell. What's gone wrong now? Captain Wilson speaking."

"Hello, captain. I bet that beer tastes good after the day you've had."

"Bloody hell," said the captain, standing up and looking around for the young fellow.

"You won't see me, captain, because I am not there."

"Where the hell are you?"

"Calm down, captain, before you have a heart attack. It's time you got to know some more about me now. Sit down and sip that beer."

The captain was fuming because he did not know what was happening.

"Right, captain, for your ears only, I am a long way from where you are, but I can see on my computer screen what has just happened in this case – you getting a cold beer and sitting down in your pergola. Now, don't ask how, because unless you were a physics master like Einstein and an electrical engineer like Nikola Tesla and a computer guru like me, you would not understand. What I have, Captain Wilson, is the ability to walk back in time and see what happened. I can see the past a second after it has happened, but I cannot see the future because it has not yet happened.

The future can change, but the past is locked in because it has happened. Do you grasp what I am saying, Captain?"

"You mean you can see what happens after it has happened, but you can't change anything?"

"That is correct, Captain, and please don't try and find out how I do this as it is very complex. I can see you have many questions, but they will need to wait."

"Who are you talking to, love?" said the captain's wife as she arrived with some cheese and biscuits.

"I have a very important call, love, so could you leave me alone until I call you?"

He was given a strange look by his wife, who turned and went back into the house.

"Sounds like you will be in trouble explaining this call. Right, captain, what do you think if I just walked into your station and personally gave you all this information and sat down at a computer and explained everything? What would happen to me?"

"Well, you would become a VIP and be on the news and in the papers as the person who gave us the information to solve this crime."

"Then what happens, captain?"

"What do you mean?"

"Every hitman and killer in Australia would be trying to kill me before I had a chance to expose their dirty crimes. Don't tell me the police would protect me as a lot of them are tied up with organised crime."

"Yes, I see where you are coming from."

"I picked you, captain, because you were involved in this crime investigation twenty-five years ago, and you have been clean all through your police career. Captain, I need the reward, so when the day comes, I can just fade away and disappear, but that takes money."

"I can see where you are coming from. What do I call you?"

"Time Walker is good enough. Now I will leave you in peace to enjoy your beer and cheese and crackers, and please keep all this to yourself."

With that, the captain was holding the phone with no body to talk to.

The captain was sitting with his head in his hands when his wife spoke to him again. "Are you OK, love?"

The captain lifted his head and, in a quiet voice, said, "I think I am having a nervous breakdown. How can I get a beer out of the fridge and sit down, and this young fellow can see what I am doing?"

"You are not making sense, love. What are you talking about?"

"Well, twenty-five years ago, before I met you, and I was just a young constable, there was a young lady abducted here in the town. The town went kind of crazy with families accusing one another, strangers to town being accused, past boyfriends and current boyfriends, the list went on and on. We followed every clue that came across the police desk, but nothing. Eventually, the search was scaled down until the whole case went cold. We have never closed the case, and at times, we have taken all the evidence we had collected out of the cupboard and went through everything all over again. It has haunted me for twenty-five years, and then out of the blue, we get a tip-off with some photos.

Then we get another tip-off about where a body was buried, and today forensic exhumed the remains of a young woman and have taken the remains back to Sydney."

"Well, that's good, love. What's the problem?"

"The young fellow who tipped us off has not been identified, and when I came home and sat down here with a beer, he rings me up and tells me that he can see me and to enjoy the beer and cheese and biscuits that you are bringing me."

"Well, why didn't you invite him in to have a beer and a talk with you?"

"Because he is not bloody here, he is somewhere else but can see everything that I do, no matter where I am or what I am doing. Tomorrow will be a nightmare as the press will have got wind of what has happened, and they will turn the whole place into a circus."

"Calm down, darling. Getting stressed about it will not help at all. Now finish your beer and nibbles and come inside."

Chapter 6
THE PRESS ARRIVE

The next morning was overcast with light rain falling. The captain took an umbrella and walked the couple of blocks from his house to the police station. He turned the corner and came to a complete stop. The area in front of the police station was filled with people milling about, and there were what appeared to be TV vans parked all up and down the road.

"Bloody hell," said the captain. "Here we go. The circus has started."

He was almost at the police station before he was spotted by the crowd. Then the melee started.

"Captain, can you give us a couple of minutes and tell us about the body you found?"

"Where did you get the information from?"

It was just a full-on cacophony of sound, which turned everything into a babble of noise. He pushed his way through the rabble and brushed aside the microphones that were thrust into his face. Finally, he made the door of the police station, which he wrenched open and pushed his way inside.

"Constable, get the traffic boys to move the TV vans which are almost blocking the road, and get some more officers to clear that rabble off the footpath and away from the front door. You can tell the reporters I will speak to them in 30 minutes if they sort themselves out and start acting like responsible reporters and not the rabble that is out there at the moment. Tell them we will have a news conference in the rear car park. You might also arrange for their press accreditation to be inspected as they come into the rear car park, otherwise we will have half the town there as well."

"Yes, sir. Right away."

The captain went into the ready room, and with a look of pure acid, asked,
"Who opened their mouth and discussed with the press what had happened here?"

A few eyes went down, as the captain expected.

"Right, from now on, it will be on a need-to-know basis. You will only be told what I think you need to know. Is that understood, everyone?"

There were a few mumbled replies. The captain stormed off into his office and slammed the door.

"Not a very good way to start the day, me old china."

Twenty-five minutes later, the captain came out of his office and went through the police station to the rear door. The press started to all speak at once until the captain roared out, "Quiet, the lot of you, or I will have you run off the premises."

In a moment, there was total silence.

"Right, everyone, keep quiet until I have finished speaking. Constable, come up here and stand with me."

In a flash, the constable was standing beside the captain.

"Right, a couple of days ago, a young fellow dressed in a hoodie, a pair of jeans with the knees out of them, and a pair of Doc Martens boots entered the foyer of the station and handed the constable here a memory stick for a computer. He only said one word: 'CAPTAIN.' The constable brought the memory stick to me. I had the IT department check for viruses, but it was clean. On playing the contents of the memory stick, we had images of an old Mazda Bongo van, which looked twenty-plus years old. We were able to get the number plate of the van, and the short video showed two men abducting a young lady." Hands went up to ask questions, but the captain immediately said, "When I am finished talking, I will answer some relevant questions."

"I was sure that I recognized some of the background in the video. I had photos made, and the constable and I went across town and walked the street where I believed the abduction took place. Now, twenty-plus years later, the trees planted by the local council are now 20 meters high. However, we could recognize the shop fronts to prove without doubt that the photos were taken there. My men checked with motor vehicle registration, and the Mazda van showed up as being stolen and found burnt out at about the same time. We are following that line of investigation now. The following day, I went to have a coffee with the mayor, and when I arrived at the coffee shop, he handed me another memory stick. The same young fellow said only the one word, 'CAPTAIN.' This memory stick went through the same procedure. However, it showed two men lifting a sack out the side door of the Bongo van and taking it into the bush.

With the help of the local president of the bushwalking club, we were able to ascertain the location of the van in the video. We got some forensic people with ground-penetrating radar and searched the area near where the van was parked. This search disclosed what we believed was a shallow grave. This assumption proved correct, and we removed the remains of what we believe was a young lady. The remains are now with the forensic department in Sydney. That is all the information that we have at this time. Now, I will answer relevant questions only if it is done in an orderly manner."

Every hand went up at once. The captain picked out a newsman from one of the national TV networks.

"Captain, do you have an identity on the remains?"

"At this time, no, as they are still being examined, and then we hope to get some DNA for a positive ID. Next."

"Captain, you say video—how is this possible when twenty years ago there were no videos?"

"Right, the video is made up of a series of photos taken very close together and made into a video. The video is grainy with some distortion, but enough to get things like the number plate on the van."

"Who is the young man you mentioned, and where did he get the video from?"

"That we do not know, as he is very elusive, and we have searched all the CCTV cameras in the vicinity where we have had contact with him, but we still cannot identify him."

"Can you identify either of the men in the videos?"

"The answer to that is no. We cannot identify either of the men, as their faces are hidden."

"That is all the questions that I am answering at this time. Please leave the police car park. Thank you."

The captain turned and walked back into the station.

"Constable, see that this lot of ghouls leave the car park, please."

"Yes, captain."

The captain turned and went back into the police station. He was just sitting down when his phone rang. He looked at the sender's name, and there was the Time Walker name.

"Good morning, young fellow. What can I do for you this morning?"

"More like what I can do for you, captain. You have really thrown the cat in amongst the pigeons, like my old dad used to say."

"What do you mean?"

"You should have pinned a target on the back of every young person wearing a hoodie, jeans, and boots. Every guilty killer will now try to knock off his would-be identifier."

"I think you are overreacting, young fellow. This is not the streets of Harlem."

"Mark my words, captain, there will be a lot of trouble over the next few days. How are you going with my reward, Captain? I have given you one victim. When you have my reward together, I will give you the faces of the killers."

The phone went dead in the captain's hands.

"Hell, this case will give me a heart attack before I am much older."

The captain punched in another number and waited.

"Commissioner? Captain Wilson here."

"I know who it is, Captain. You've got a right circus on your hands out there in the bush. Good work on finding the remains, and we are sending through the names of the mothers of the missing girls so you can get them to come in for DNA testing."

"Commissioner, what is the status of the reward money? The young bloke who has given us all this information has said that he will give us the IDs of the killers when the reward is ready to be paid."

"Well, the pollies are dragging their feet on this, just like they do on everything. They are trying to work out how they can get some political mileage out of the whole shebang. I will ring the Premier again today and remind him that it was his party that promised the reward years ago. You can't get the young bloke to come into the station and work with you?"

"Not a chance, commissioner. He is as shy as, and doesn't want his face or name in any of the papers. He's got a valid reason that he will become a target for every crim in the state not wanting to be exposed."

"Captain, how did he get the photos of the abduction and the burial of the victim? That was twenty-five years ago, and he wasn't even born?"

"Commissioner, all he told me was you need to be part Einstein, part Tesla, part electrical engineer, and a computer guru to get the answer. He lost me when he started talking like that."

"All right, I will chase the pollies up again. We need this reward to find out just who the guilty parties are. Leave it with me, captain."

The captain hung up just as there was a knock at the door. "Come in."

"Hello, sergeant. What can I do for you?"

"Well, captain, off the record, what is happening around here?"

"What do you mean, sergeant? The boys in blue getting curious?"

"Captain, the town is going mad. Last night we had fights in three of the pubs in town. One of them took six of my uniformed boys to break it up, and two of the would-be world champions are in the slammer waiting to go before the beak this morning. They will get a slap on the wrist, but a night in the cells should wake them up a bit."

"Sergeant, this is what the town was like twenty-five years ago when the girls disappeared. Families accusing other families, fathers accusing boyfriends. Total madness, but there is nothing we can do except try to keep a lid on it with a visible presence by your boys in blue. If it gets too much, I will request some more troops from Sydney. Best I can do for you, Sarge."

"Thanks, captain. I will go have a talk to the day shift before they hit the streets."

"On your way out, send in the constable from the front desk for me. I have another job for her."

A few minutes later, there was another knock on the door. "Come in, constable, and take a seat."

"Right, here is a list of the parents of the two girls who disappeared and their last known addresses. Take one of the detectives with you, and have one of each set of parents come in with you to the medical centre downtown and have them give a sample for a DNA test so we can identify whose daughter we found out there in the bush. I have asked for you, as you can imagine what this is going to be like for the parents after all this time, so be gentle with them."

"Will do, captain."

"When you get done, come and let me know where we are at. OK?"

"Yes, sir."

"I am hoping that forensics can find some DNA to identify the remains. I am handing you a nasty job, constable, but if anyone can get the samples, it is you."

The constable left the office with the addresses of the parents. The captain sat at his desk for a while, just trying to sort everything out in his head.

Chapter 7

THE FIRST VISIT TO HILL TOP FARM

The captain had just settled himself down when his mobile phone rang.

A quick glance was enough to see that it was the Time Walker ringing him again.

Before he could say a word, the young fellow spoke. "Well, good morning, Captain. Have you decided which Magistrate you are going to ask to give you a search warrant?"

"Yes, Justice Wilmot, if you are happy with that?"

"No worries, Captain, he is a straight shooter. Now, do you know the property Hill Top? Of course, you do; you used to go out there with the footy team and have barbecues and piss-ups, didn't you?"

"Yes, we did. The whole footy team did. What else don't you know about me?" The captain replied angrily.

"Nothing about you, Captain. I know all about you, which is why I am helping you. Now ring the magistrate, get a search warrant, and get a couple of cars of the boys in blue out there ASAP before any evidence gets destroyed because the killers are getting ready to go out there to burn the old sheds and the old homestead to the ground to get rid of any evidence. Better get the forensic boys as well, as all the evidence you need is still there, but not for much longer. Goodbye, Captain."

The captain was sitting there looking at a dead phone.

The captain burst out of the office and called for the police sergeant.

The police sergeant was there in a moment.

"What's up, Captain?"

"Sergeant, get two cars with some of your people and get out to the property Hill Top and secure the property. Don't let anyone onto the property. I will have a search warrant as soon as possible. Now make this happen immediately before all the evidence goes up in smoke. You know where the property is?"

"Yes, sir, on our way."

The sergeant turned and was gone in an instant. A couple of minutes later, two cars went out of the rear yard with sirens howling and lights flashing.

The captain went back to his office and sat down. He opened his phone to the contacts, looked up Justice Wilmot's number, and pressed the button.

The phone was answered almost immediately. "Hello, Bill, what can I do for you? Been a while since I heard from you. I see you have been very busy of late."

"Yes, Thomas. Mate, I need a search warrant for a farm in relation to the remains we dug up the other day. I have received a tip-off that there is evidence on the farm pertaining to the girls' murder. That's the best I can say at this time."

"Well, Bill, I have known you for a long time, and you have always been a straight shooter, so send one of your detectives over and pick the search warrant up. Send the address with him, and I will have the rest of the paperwork done by the time he gets here."

"Thanks, Thomas, the tips I have received to date have all been good, and I hope this one is as well. Thanks for your assistance, mate."

The captain ended the call and went to the door. "Detective Browning, grab a car and go to the courthouse and find Justice Wilmot. He will have a search warrant for you. Bring it back here immediately." He handed a scrap of paper to the detective.

"This is the address of the premises. You other two guys, get some forensic equipment and put it into the van. I have a tip-off that I want to follow up on."

There was muttering of yes, sir's as they all headed out to the car park.

Half an hour later, Detective Browning was back at the station with the search warrant in his hand. "Got it here, Captain."

"Right, grab a box of drinking water, and let's go."

Just as they headed out to the cars, the captain's phone rang. It was the Time Walker.

"Captain Wilson, how are you today?"

"Busy as you well know."

"I see that you have a search warrant and the boys in blue are now arriving at the property. If I had left it another couple of hours, there would have been some fires out there, and a lot of evidence would have disappeared."

"I will call you when you get to the property, Captain."

The phone went dead.

They were getting into the two vehicles, and the young detective asked the captain, "Is that your mystery tip-off, young fellow, Captain?"

"You just drive the car and let me answer the phone, OK?"

"Sorry, Captain."

The phone rang again as they pulled out of the driveway.

"Sergeant Timms, Captain. We have secured the farm. There is nobody here. The whole place is deserted."

"Yes, Sergeant, it was abandoned years ago after the old fellow died. There are a few useless kids who have been fighting over the property ever since. I am on my way out there now, so just wait until I get there. Keep the squad car hidden and sit quietly just in case anyone comes into the place."

"OK, Captain."

The news people were calling out, "What's happening, Captain?"

When he did not reply, they all started running to their vehicles so they could follow the police vehicles.

The two vehicles sped along the back road heading out of town. Their flashing lights on, but the sirens were silent.

A kilometre back was a small convoy of reporters and TV people trying to keep the police vehicles in sight.

The driver spoke. "Looks like every reporter in the state is chasing us, Captain."

The captain was silent as well, leaning against the door pillar, hoping the Time Walker was not making a fool of him. His head was full of questions but no answers. He took out his phone, checked he had a signal, and then punched in the commissioner's number. "The phone only rang once before it was answered.

"Hello, Captain. What's happening?"

"Commissioner, what is happening with the reward money?"

"Bloody pollies are still fart-arsing around. What is happening? Has the young bloke been in touch again?"

"Commissioner, we are heading out to a property with a search warrant based upon a tip-off from the young bloke that there was evidence there that would be destroyed if we did not act quickly. I am not sure if I am being led along by the nose, but I could not take the chance, and his tip-offs have been accurate to date. If this tip-off is accurate, he is going to ask me what is happening with the reward. This is his disappearing money if things go public, and he needs to hide out, so he will not be happy if he has been honest with us and we have not been as honest with him."

"I know what you mean, Captain. Pollies are quick to make promises, but when the time comes to pay the piper, they are all into trying to get out of it. I will shake the tree again and see what happens. Try and keep the young bloke on side while I try and get his reward money sorted out. Keep me informed on what you find out there."

The phone went dead.

"Bloody public servants are the same all over."

"What's that, Captain?"

44

"Nothing, young fellow. Not much further and you will see a road turning off to the left. Take that for about 50 meters and stop. We will bring one of the traffic vehicles out to block the road to keep the ghouls out. See that big tree? Turn left there and go about 30 meters and stop."

The car slowed and turned left off the country road.

The captain picked up the radio mike and called the sergeant. "Send one of those marked patrol cars up here, Sarge."

One of the cars pulled away from where it was parked and headed for the gate. The forensic van pulled up alongside the captain. "What do you want us to do, Captain?"

"Go down there to where the cars are parked and wait for me, OK?"

They pulled away, and the patrol car pulled up alongside the unmarked captain's car. "What would you like us to do, Captain?"

"Right. Block off the access road into the farm and make sure these ghouls park correctly alongside the road. If they give you any trouble, threaten them with a night in the cells."

"Will do, Captain." The police car arrived at the entrance just as the first reporter's car started to turn into the farm property.

The patrol car blocked the road, and the two patrolmen got out and walked up to the news car.

"Back out and park correctly alongside the road, otherwise you will be wearing a traffic fine." The driver backed out, grumbling all the while.

Next moment, there were another dozen cars and vans parking anywhere, so the officers walked along telling them to park correctly and leave the road clear for rural traffic, or else.

There was much toing and froing, and then there was a crowd of press people all wanting to know what was happening.

"I have no idea. I just follow orders, and if anyone thinks they will walk in, then they will be arrested and spend some time in the cells. Is that understood by everyone?"

There was a babble of voices, but the officer just turned and walked off, leaving the 5th estate frustrated and angry.

Chapter 8

THE AXE HANDLES

The captain's car parked alongside the sergeant's vehicle, and the captain got out.

"Who has that box of water?"

A bottle appeared, and the captain opened it and took a swallow.

"Don't ask, Sarge. I don't know what we are doing here. However, here we are, so make the best of it. Let's have a look in the various sheds here. It all seems different from what I remember from twenty-five years ago."

The sergeant and the forensic people joined the captain as they wandered across to the old bush sheds.

"Look out for Joe Blakes, that is, snakes to you young people. They just love this sort of environment."

The first shed had no doors and must have been used for the storage of hay, as there were still remnants of a couple of bales of fodder. The Sarge gave it a kick, and mice ran out.

"Food for the snakes, Captain."

"Sarge, I have no idea what we are doing here, so please, no questions."

A quick look around, and they moved over to the small room at the end of the hay shed.

The door was just about fallen off its hinges, so the captain gave it a good pull and stepped aside as it fell to the ground.

"These old bush sheds are all at the ends of their lifespans."

Getting a stick, the captain swiped away some spider webs, and the pair looked into what appeared to be an old tack room with an old bridle and a busted saddle. Some old hand tools hung on hooks. The purpose of some of them was a mystery. The sergeant turned on his phone light and shone it around the inside of the room. Some old axes and handles hung on the walls, an old table rotting away in the middle of the room; otherwise, not much else to attract attention.

The captain gave a shiver.

"What's up, Captain? Feeling cold?"

"No, Sarge. But there is evil in this room. I can feel it."

The captain walked back out to his car, having a drink as he walked along.

The looks on the faces of the officers and forensic people were enough to tell him that they thought he was losing his mind from all the recent stress.

He opened the car door and sat down, drinking some water and slowing his thoughts down.

He could feel the evil in the air after 25 years of dealing with the dregs of the human race.

Just then, he felt the buzzing of his phone in his pocket.

Taking his phone out, he saw it was from the Time Walker.

"Good morning, young fellow. Well, you have me out here on the farm where I had a lot of good times when I was a young footy player 30 years ago, but I can feel evil here."

"Sorry to be a bit late, Captain, but it's hard for me to follow fast cars. However, we are all here now, including the ghouls at the gate. Captain, get your forensic techs to go over to the old shed where you just were and look at the back wall. You will see two old axe handles.

That is not linseed oil on the handles, Captain, but human blood. They were soaked in the young girl's blood. Get them to do a test while you are here. Treat them with reverence; they were used for inflicting a lot of pain and suffering. That old table as well needs to be tested, and the dirt floor is soaked in pain and suffering also."

The phone went off, and the captain was alone with his thoughts.

"Sarge, get the forensic people and some large plastic bags."

The captain walked back to the tack shed and waited for the forensic people.

There, on the back wall, tucked behind a wall brace, were two old axe handles.

The two technicians from forensics arrived with an assortment of plastic bags.

"Yes, Captain?"

"Gloves on and collect those two old axe handles. Take them back to your van and do a quick test on them and tell me if that's blood— those dark stains. Take some photos first so we can prove where they came from. This is a crime scene now."

The techs nodded their heads and went and drove their van almost up to the shed and got to work.

The captain and the sergeant walked back to their cars.

"The captain is losing it, I reckon," said one of the techs very quietly to the other tech.

"Let's just do as he asks, then we can all go home," said the other, as he got out a camera and started taking photos of the outside of the shed, then through the door, and a series of photos of the inside of the tack room.

They dressed in disposable overalls and booties, donned gloves, and then went and collected the two old axe handles. Without touching anything else, they set up the awning alongside the van, got their gear out, and started doing a test on a small section of one of the axe handles.

The captain sat by himself and finished off the bottle of water. He could see the looks on all the faces. He had lost his marbles and had had a nervous breakdown. The captain got another bottle of water and started to drink it. Time moved slowly.

The test seemed to take forever, then the senior of the two technicians came across to the captain.

"Well, am I going nuts, or have you found anything?"

"Human blood, Captain. Faint, but still there. This is now a crime scene, so we will get the guys to barricade it all off."

"Right. I think you will find blood on the table as well as the floor. I am going back to town but will leave a squad car here, and I will send out some food and refreshments. I will also contact Sydney and get some assistance for you. You have a big job ahead of you to test everything in that room and then test the hay shed and the old house. If you need anything, then call me and I will arrange it. OK?"

The captain turned to his driver. "Back to town and not a word to those ghouls at the gate."

The car turned and drove off.

"Well, I thought the captain was losing the plot, but he is a long way in front of us. The murder weapons are still here after twenty-five years."

"I am amazed as well," said the second techie.

"The story is he has somebody sending him tip-offs."

"I don't know, but we have done more crime solving in the last week than we have all last year. Right, let's get to it."

Chapter 9

THE DEMISE OF THE POLICE MINISTER

The captain sat back in the car seat and closed his eyes. The next moment, he was startled by the news people all banging on the car doors and roof, shouting questions.

The captain rolled down the window and roared at the horde, "Next person to bang the car gets a night in jail. Is that understood?"

Silence reigned. "Right, I will give you all some information when I get back to the police station. Now, everyone get out of the way."

The crowd parted, and the captain's driver sped off.

"Bloody uneducated, ill-mannered bunch if ever I saw anyone."

The driver kept his silence as the captain was getting a very short fuse lately. Better to say nothing and not draw the wrath of the boss down on you.

The ride back to town was done in silence.

The police car pulled into the station yard, and the captain got out and went to his office.

The constable followed him through the office and was given the nod to take a seat.

"Okay, constable, how did your day go to date?"

"Well, sir, I was able to find both sets of parents, and they were stunned, to say the least. But they all came with us to the hospital and gave a sample for the DNA testing. They are all now waiting to see what the laboratory comes up with."

"Well, constable, we might have found the murder weapons today while you were out of the station. They were found on a property some miles out of town. Now my driver knows where the property is, so could you speak to him, get some food for everyone who is out there, plus more drinking water and whatever else you think of, and take it out to them as the farm is now a designated crime scene."

"No worries, captain."

"Thanks."

The constable stood up and lingered for a moment.

"Captain, are you okay with what is happening?"

"To be honest, constable, no. I am not, but what can I do? This young fellow is drip-feeding me information, and to date, it has all been accurate. I just don't know what is coming next. I hate not knowing where we are going; however, he is solving a twenty-five-year-old missing person case that we didn't have a clue about what happened."

"Captain, if I may say something, just go with what the young bloke gives you and try not to stress out too much. Everyone here is behind you one hundred percent."

The captain nodded. "Thanks, constable. Your kind words are a big help to me at this time."

The constable left the captain alone, and he closed his eyes and tried to get his thoughts in order. In such a short time, they had found the remains of a victim, seen the vehicle that she was abducted in, and where she was abducted. Now they were searching the probable murder location and finding the possible murder weapons. For a case 25 years old, this was awesome progress.

The captain punched in the commissioner's number in Sydney and waited while it rang.

The wait was short, and the commissioner came on the phone almost immediately. "Captain, what news have you got for me?"

The captain gave him a rundown on the visit to the farm and what was found there.

There was silence from the commissioner. "Right, I will send up another forensic team, plus a few more boys in blue to help out with traffic control around the crime scene."

The captain nodded; however, he was nodding to himself as the commissioner had hung up.

The captain stood up and went out to the lunchroom, made himself a mug of tea, and went back to his office.

He was just taking the first sip of lemon tea when his phone rang. He glanced at the caller and saw it was his mate, the Time Walker.

"Hello, captain, me again. How are you?"

"Stressed, young fellow. The people around here are starting to think I am going around the twist, dragging them out into the bush to an old farm shed. However, your information was correct. The axe handles were stained in human blood."

"Right, captain, I know you are trying hard to get my reward, and you are being fobbed off, so don't be surprised what happens in Sydney over the next few days. Now, I want you to get a backhoe from the council with a drain-cleaning bucket out to the farm tomorrow morning when the forensic team arrives from Sydney. Can you arrange that?"

"Of course I can, but why do you want a backhoe?"

"You will find out tomorrow, captain. Sorry to stress you out so much, but I like you, captain. Goodbye." And the captain was sitting there with his tea going cold and a dead phone in his hand.

"Constable, can you come in here for a moment?"

"Yes, captain. Can I help?"

"Yes, can you contact the local council and see if we can get a backhoe with a drain-cleaning bucket out to the farm when the forensics team arrives tomorrow?"

"I am on my way, captain."

"Thanks."

He went to take a sip of his tea and found it stone cold. He put it down in disgust.

The captain could hear the noise building in the police carpark at the rear of the station.

"Bloody hell, I forgot about the rabble. Well, I need to sort them out."

The captain headed out through the ready room.

"You two guys come with me," he indicated as he went through the ready room.

The three detectives headed out to the car park.

The three stood on the back steps. "All right, what can I do for you people now?"

A cacophony of sound arose from the car park. "One at a time, please."

"Captain, why are your people out at that farm where you all went this morning?"

"Right, I received a tip-off that there had been a crime committed there, so we naturally investigated."

Another babble of voices broke out.

"Quiet. Now, another question."

"Captain, what did you find there?"

"Right, we did find some evidence relating to a crime, so the area is now out of bounds to anyone not officially related to the investigation."

"Yes, but what did you find?"

"Ladies and Gentlemen of the press, I am not at liberty to disclose that information yet, as it is still under investigation. That is all that I am able to disclose to you at this time. Please leave the carpark and please park your car in accordance with the traffic regulations. Thank you."

The three detectives turned and went back into the police station. "Get a couple of uniformed men to get this rabble back out onto the street."

"Yes, sir."

Everyone was walking around the Captain on tiptoe as he was very grouchy at the moment. They all thought that he should be on top of the world with all the exposures that had happened in the last week.

The captain went back to his office and closed the door.

The people in the station knew better than to disturb him when the door was closed unless it was an emergency.

The day passed slowly for the captain as he was expecting another call at any time. Knock-off time finally arrived, and the staff made their way back to the station.

"Sergeant."

"Yes, sir."

"Is there a car stationed at the farm for the night? We need some security; otherwise, we will have those news people trooping around making a mess."

"Already arranged, sir. Car and two officers."

"Good. There should be some additional uniformed people here first up in the morning to assist you. I have a feeling that that farm is about to get a whole lot busier tomorrow."

"Yes, sir."

"Right, let's all go and get a good night's rest."

The station slowly wound down until just the night shift was on duty.

The captain grabbed his umbrella and walked out of the station. There was only one news crew still there, and the interviewer came running over to the captain. The captain kept on walking and held up his hand. The press guy fell into step alongside him, and before he could say a word, the captain spoke.

"I have no information for you at this time, like I said earlier today. We are investigating a crime, and until we have more information from forensics, then I have no info for you. Now, please leave me to walk home in peace."

The press guy dropped off and left the captain to walk on with his shoulders down and deep in thought.

He arrived home and went to the fridge and grabbed a beer. His wife walked into the kitchen and said, "Hello, dear. Would you like some cheese and crackers brought out to you, to the pergola?"

"Be nice, love. Come and join me for a while before the sun goes down completely. The sunsets are always nice at this time of the year."

The captain made his way out to the pergola and sat down, took a swig of beer, and undid his tie.

Just then, his phone rang.

"Bloody hell, not my mate, please."

Glancing at the caller ID, he saw it was the Time Walker.

"Hello, young fellow, what can I do for you now?"

A cheery voice said, "Hello, Captain. Just giving you a heads-up. Watch the news tonight. The State Premier will be looking for a new police minister, as the current one has been feeding information to the crime gangs in Sydney for a brown paper bag or two. He is the person who has been holding up my reward money, so now he can find out what it is like to see the inside of a cell for a while."

"You are not joking, are you, Time Walker?"

"No. I thought it was about time to have a look at the main man, and sure enough, he has his hand in the cookie jar. Well, good night, captain, you can sleep tight as you are a good person."

Just at that moment, the captain's wife walked into the pergola.

"Are you talking to your young friend again, dear?"

"Yes, love. We need to watch the news tonight, as he has told me that the police minister will be arrested for corruption."

"What, another high-up person in trouble?"

"Yes, darling, it seems that their big salaries are never enough for some of these people. Let's take our drinks and nibbles and go watch the news."

The couple had just entered their lounge and turned on the TV news channel when the announcer spoke about the police minister being accused of corruption. There was a video showing the minister talking to the boss of one of the bikie gangs, then that went onto him talking to one of the Asian criminal gangs. In both of them, he was seen receiving a parcel of money and putting it into his coat pocket.

The captain immediately recognized the video as coming from the Time Walker.

"Do you think that is a genuine video, dear?"

"Without a doubt, darling. They won't be able to prove that is not the genuine article."

Just at that moment, his phone rang. A quick glance showed it was the police commissioner calling.

"Commissioner."

"Are you watching the news, captain?"

"Yes, sir. Looks like you will have a new boss in the near future."

"Do you reckon those videos are the real McCoy, captain?"

"Without a doubt, commissioner. You might start chasing up the reward money in a day or so for my young friend. He tipped me off that something was going to happen in Sydney in the near future. He was not wrong."

"So, unless the premier finds the money, he might find himself in trouble as well."

"Always possible, Commissioner. We owe the young fellow his reward, and he has been very helpful showing us the suspected murder weapons, and still, the police minister did not want to pay the reward. The young fellow has asked for a backhoe for tomorrow morning out at the farm. I suspect he will show us another burial site, which is way over what he promised. I will let you know what happens as I get more information, but you should ask for a meeting with the Premier about the rewards. We advertised them, so we are obligated to pay them if the information provided is correct."

"I agree with you, Captain. I will chase up the Premier tomorrow morning. The extra people you have requested are on their way. Good night, Captain."

The phone went dead.

"He is another political animal always covering his arse."

"I know, dear, you've told me that a hundred times, but it is what it is."

The captain picked up his beer and went back to his seat in the pergola. Muttering to himself, "I wonder what tomorrow is going to bring. The news mob are growing by the hour. The locals are restless because they know that in amongst them is a killer, and they have no idea who it is. I have no idea what is happening, as the young fellow is running the show. I am just a puppet on his strings." Night fell, and the captain's mood had not improved.

Chapter 10

DEALING WITH THE PRESS

The captain was awake at daylight.

He headed for the bathroom for a quick shower as he had had a troubled night's sleep.

He turned the coffee maker on as he passed the kitchen—one of the few modern appliances that he approved of.

The shower was over almost before it started. The captain felt driven this morning to get to the office. He knew it was going to be a full-on day. He grabbed a vacuum cup and made himself a double shot of black coffee, two spoons of sugar, and jammed the lid on.

He was dressed even before his wife had surfaced from a deep sleep.

He was heading out the door as his wife called to him to calm down; the day was still young.

"Yes, dear."

The captain did not notice the birds singing or the sun shining through the early morning mist as he strode off towards the police station, mumbling to himself.

He rounded the corner and could not believe his eyes. The street in front of the police station was jam-packed with cars and milling reporters.

The crowd, at that moment, spied the captain coming down the street, and like a pack of hounds chasing a fox, they all charged toward the captain, shouting questions while they were still 50 meters away.

It was such a babble of voices mixed together that any sentence was unrecognizable. However, the captain knew what was being asked.

He put his head down and ploughed through them like an icebreaker through pack ice until he had made it up the steps of the station, at which point he stopped and turned to face the rabble with his two arms in the air.

"Quiet!" he bellowed. His voice silenced them, and before they could start again, he spoke.

"One at a time. You," he said, pointing to a young lady with a microphone in her outstretched hand.

"Captain, could you tell us what you found out at the farm where your forensic people were working the whole day?"

"Yes, we found a couple of axe handles that had old blood stains on them. These have been sent to the state laboratory in Sydney for further examination."

"Next, you, young fellow."

"Captain, we understand that you have requested a backhoe from the council to go there today. Can you tell us why?"

"Yes, there are a couple of suspicious areas that we want to excavate to see if there is anything buried there."

"Next. You, Peter." He indicated an older man who was holding a microphone.

"Are we talking about a serial killer here, Captain?"

"Peter, at this time, we are still investigating and awaiting forensic information. That's all the information I can give you. Now, everyone,

I want this street cleared of cars and people. Otherwise, I will have my people start arresting you for obstruction. I will hold another press conference at 6 p.m. this evening in the car park at the rear of the station. Good morning."

The captain turned and went into the station to a howl of voices, all calling out questions from the mob of reporters.

The inside of the station was like a sanctuary compared to the bloodhounds outside.

"Good morning, constable. You're in early this morning."

The female constable nodded to the captain. "I think we're in for a full day, captain."

"Yes. What's the word on the backhoe?"

"It should be there in about an hour, captain."

"Right, get somebody to relieve you on the front counter, speak to the sergeant, and let's get a meeting going in the squad room."

"Yes, sir."

The captain turned and walked to the squad room. All the detectives were there, as he expected. None wanted to miss out on what was happening within the investigation.

Chapter 11

EVIL ON THE FARM

The captain made himself a new coffee and sat at the front of the room.

Within minutes, the room had filled.

"Right, a quick report, Sergeant, on what is happening around the town?"

"Well, Captain, things are still powder keg at the moment. A few beers, and they all start arguing over this case we are working on."

"Well, it is about to get worse when they find out we have a council backhoe going out there to do some digging. Where are the forensic guys?"

"Well, they worked till dark and went back out there at first light this morning. I still have a patrol car and two constables who were there all night. Another pair have gone out there to relieve them for the day shift."

"Right, we have more people coming up from Sydney this morning. More forensic and more uniform boys. Let's hope we have a good day. Sarge, send the forensic people out as soon as they arrive. Constable, organize drinking water and food for everyone, then get a driver and vehicle from the uniform branch and come out there. I want you detectives to come out there so we can get a better understanding of what has happened there and a timeline of when, so you guys and ladies can start finding out the previous owners and who has used the farm in the past. Any questions?"

"Right, let's go there now and get started. Sarge, see if you can get some discipline out of this rabble out the front."

The room started to empty, and within minutes, cars started to roll out of the parking lot.

This set off a scramble amongst the reporters as they headed for their vans and cars.

The sound of a news helicopter passed overhead. The captain just shook his head and settled in for the thirty-minute drive to the farm.

As the captain turned into the farm 30 minutes later, the convoy of police vehicles and reporters' vans stretched for over a kilometre. The captain picked up the radio microphone and spoke, "Sarge, make sure your people keep this rabble out of the crime scene and are parked correctly off the side of the road. I don't want any car accidents with locals and these people. That would just aggravate any problems we have already."

"Understood, Captain."

The captain indicated to the driver to park in the shade of a big tree growing there. He got out and walked across to the forensic team, stopping short and calling out to the team leader.

"Good morning, people. Can you give me a heads up on your progress yesterday?"

The team leader came across to where the captain was standing.

"Well, Captain, the tack room is where all the violence was used against any victim. We have found traces of blood on the axe handles that we dispatched to Sydney lab last night. We have found the same traces on the table and that was wrapped in plastic and sent as well.

There were some old leather belts showing the same traces, and they have gone also.

We have gone over the old house and the hay storage area, but they were both free of any traces, so all we have is what is in the tack room. Captain, why have we got a backhoe here?"

The captain was asking himself that, as the young fellow had not told him why he needed a backhoe.

"All in good time, people."

The captain walked away and wandered around the back of the shed. He walked about 50 meters and took out his phone to check the signal.

The phone rang. The time walker symbol came up, and the captain let out his breath.

"Good morning, young fellow."

"Sorry, Captain, I had a bit of sleep in. Been busy last night nailing that police minister who is trying to weasel his way out of the charges. Captain, look to your left and you will see a large hole full of rubbish. This is where all the empty beer cans and bottles ended up over the years. Now clean the rubbish out and be careful because under all of this, you will find the last resting place of another young lady. She deserves a proper burial and not just thrown out like the rubbish. Keep the backhoe on site. I will tell you where to go next. We will talk later today, Captain."

The phone went dead. The captain slipped the phone into his pocket and walked towards the rubbish pit.

He could feel a wave of sadness pass over him as he got closer. The pit was almost full to the surface, and the feeling was very intense as he stood looking at the rubbish.

"We are coming for you, my dear, and I will find the people who did this and make them pay."

The captain turned and walked back towards the forensic team and his own people.

The captain brushed away a tear and gruffly gave some orders.

"Right, get the backhoe and clean all the rubbish out of that excavation. Put it all on one side of the pit so forensic can go through it on the off chance there is any information for us there.

When it is all out, have the operator dig very carefully under the direction of the forensic people, as I expect we will find the remains of another young lady down there, and she deserves our respect. Is that understood?"

There was a nodding of heads as the captain walked away. He could feel the tears rolling down his cheeks and made no effort to wipe them away.

"The same female constable was there and she spoke. "Captain, are you okay?"

"Yes, just thinking of a young life snuffed out by some vile evil people. I want them and I want to see them spend the rest of their lives rotting in prison before all this is over."

The captain looked up to see the sergeant coming across as well.

"Hello, Captain, are you OK?"

"All good, Sergeant, just a touch of old age, I think."

"I don't think so, Captain, but let's call it that for the moment."

"Sarge, can you get all the detectives over here for a bit of a round table?"

"No worries, boss."

In a few minutes, the whole team of detectives was standing in front of the captain.

"Right, people, I want you to find every person who has had anything to do with this farm over the last 30 years. I used to come out here and we would have piss-ups, but that was more than 30 years ago when I played football. I want to know all the owners. I want everything that has ever happened here. If somebody had cattle or sheep here on agistment, then I want to know. Anyone who rented the house, went horse riding here, I want to know. Is that understood?"

Heads nodded. They could see that the captain was getting deeply involved in this case, and all wanted to help out.

"Right, on your way and start a hard copy file on everything that you learn. Has that other team of forensic people arrived yet, Sarge?"

"Not yet, Captain."

"Well, have them work with the team we have here on that garbage dump, and I want some of your men to do a full search out to 500 metres from where we are standing and look for slight depressions in the ground, and we will get the forensic people to do a ground penetrating radar search of anything that looks like something could be buried. I can feel evil everywhere I walk on this place, and I want the bastards who did this evil."

Chapter 12

THE VAN SHOOTING

The sergeant started getting his people organized in a straight line out from where the captain was standing. "Ten meters apart and take it slowly. I can still see where they ripped the phone line on my place, and that was more than 20 years ago, so a grave site should still be visible."

The police officers strung out and started moving away from the captain.

"Keep them busy, sarge. There is more evidence buried here for us to find."

"Yes, Captain."

"Where is that driver of mine? Constable Wilkens, over here for a minute."

"Yes, Captain."

"Constable, drive me back to town, please. I have a conference call with the police commissioner in a couple of hours."

The pair climbed into the Hyundai van and headed for the gate. Immediately, the news people were out of their vehicles and clamouring for information.

"Constable, stop just short of running over the buggers, and I will get out and give them some news."

"Yes, Sir."

The car slowed to a halt just before the gate. The two traffic branch officers stood between them and the captain.

It was impossible to understand what was being said with 20 or so people all talking at once.

"Quiet!" roared the Captain.

Silence reigned.

"Right, you. What is your question?"

"Captain, what is the backhoe digger looking for?"

"The digger is removing the rubbish out of a rubbish pit, as we believe that there are remains of a body buried there. Forensic will go through all the rubbish on the off chance that there is any information still there. I expect this to take most of the day, and I will pass on any information at the press conference this evening. There is another forensic team coming from Sydney this morning to assist the current team working here. There are also more traffic police coming to keep you people in line. That is all I have to say at this time; now move out of the way, as I have a meeting in town to attend."

The rabble moved away, and the constable drove out of the farm and turned towards town.

They were taking it easy on the dirt road and just approaching the embankment to the bridge that spanned the river when the windscreen exploded in front of them.

The constable was shocked when another hole appeared beside the first one. The constable flicked the steering wheel into a tight left turn off the road and down the embankment. The van crashed through some small saplings, then she turned the van parallel to the road and said, "Brake, brake, brake!" The van lurched to a halt. "Out of the car, captain, and lay flat on the ground." The constable undid her seat belt, pulled the door open, and sprung out of the van, then lay on the ground.

The captain was lying across the van below the dash with the car's radio microphone in his hand. He was unclipping his seat belt while fumbling with the radio.

"Sarge, sarge. Anyone near the sarge, this is the Captain. We are under rifle fire near the bridge. Anyone copy?"

One of the detectives who had left the farm last came on the radio.

"Detective Johnson, Captain. What's happening?"

"What's your position, Johnson?"

"About 600 meters on the east side of the bridge, Captain."

"Right, block the road and don't let anyone through. Take cover, as there is a shooter with a high-powered rifle taking shots at us. Find some good cover and stay there until I get back to you."

"Yes, sir."

The sergeant came onto the radio straight away.

"Captain, sarge here. I have sent a car along the road to the rear of the news people to stop them from driving back into town for a look-see."

"Good one, Sergeant. Block the road off for the local traffic as well. Now, do we have a high-powered rifle with a scope in any of the police vehicles?"

"Yes, Captain, and one of the guys is a member of the gun club and a good shot over 600 meters."

"Right, Sergeant, get him up towards the bridge, but have him stop short at least 600 meters before the bridge approaches and find some decent cover. Scope out the tree line to the west and south of the bridge. That's where the shots came from. Especially look up in the trees for a sniper. This shooter is a bloody good shot, and I don't want anyone taking any risks. I also want a sharpshooter on the town side of the bridge where Detective Johnson is. Same deal, keep them back from the bridge at least 600 meters and scope out the country while I get some reinforcements from Sydney. I don't want anyone sneaking up on us while we get some assistance."

"Will do, Captain."

The captain called out to the constable. "How are you going out there, constable? Are you OK?"

"Yes, Captain, but some evil people are trying to stop us from finding them out."

"Well, find the best cover and stay down while I organize some assistance from Sydney."

The captain slid his phone out of his pocket and called the commissioner in Sydney.

The phone rang twice before being answered.

"Good morning, Captain. Is it a lovely day out there?"

"Well, commissioner, it was until we took two rifle shots through the front windscreen of the van, and we are pinned down, unable to move without exposing ourselves."

"What! Is this happening now?"

"We need some help out here, commissioner, some people who are trained for this sort of problem and with the right weapons."

The captain could hear the commissioner calling for his assistant. "Get a chopper and a tactical response team on the way now out to the captain. They have been attacked by a shooter with shots fired through a police vehicle by a long rifle. Get them into the air as soon as possible, as the captain is pinned down in a vehicle."

The commissioner came back onto the line. "Captain, are you there?"

"Yes, sir, thank you. We will stay where we are until the response team arrives. The sergeant is arranging for rifle cover of the constable and myself to make sure that nobody sneaks up on us. The van is a bit dinged up as we took two rounds through the front windscreen, which passed between the constable and myself, so we drove off the embankment to put the embankment between the shooter and us. Now it's just waiting until the professionals get here so we can finally stand up again."

"The chopper is just lifting off now, Captain, so a little under an hour should see them on the ground."

"Commissioner, another piece of news. We think we have found another grave on this farm under an old rubbish tip. The forensic people are excavating it now. I will keep you informed as we are looking for other grave sites around the farmhouse."

"Sounds like we have a serial killer on our hands. What have they been doing for the last 25 years? Good work, Captain."

"Commissioner, we have the Time Walker to thank for all this information."

"I know, Captain, and I am meeting the premier later today to push him into agreeing to pay our debts. Please keep me informed and stay safe."

The phone went dead.

"Captain?"

"Yes, constable, how can I help? We have some water here if you are thirsty, but don't stand up, whatever you do."

"No, Captain. Who is the Time Walker? Is this the young bloke who walked into the station that morning and left the memory stick?"

"Yes, constable, but that is between you and I and the commissioner, no one else."

"I understand, Captain, but why do you call him the Time Walker?"

"Because he has discovered a way to look back into time. He can't see the future because, as he said, that has not happened yet, but the past has happened and he can look at it but cannot change it in any way. This is a very strange thing, and for some reason, he likes me and helps out with these unsolved crimes because he hates evil. Well, that evil has tried to kill us this morning. I believe that these evil people believe that if they get rid of me, then they will not be exposed."

"Well, Captain, they came close to getting rid of the pair of us."

"I am sorry about that, Constable. I never meant to expose you to any danger."

"Not your fault, Captain, but when we finally round them up, I would like a few minutes with the shooter in the boxing ring at the gym."

"Well, not much longer to wait, and the chopper will be here. I have heard the sergeant talking to their team leader, and he is getting his boys spread out across the tree line in case the shooter goes that way when he hears the chopper coming in."

It was not long after that they heard a helicopter in the distance coming in fast and low. It flashed past where the Captain and the constable were pinned down, then went into a hover just above the ground near the river. Six heavily armed tactical response personnel jumped out of the chopper, dispersed in a line parallel to the river, and went to ground. The chopper lifted off and rose in the air to act as a spotter for the troops.

In a series of rushes, the troops covered the open ground and were into the tree line.

The captain was listening in to the radio chatter between the troop leader, his people, and the sarge.

Thirty minutes went by, and the troop leader came on the radio and gave the all-clear.

The captain spoke into the mic. "Give me a situation report, please. This is Captain Wilson."

"OK, Captain. We found the tree that he was shooting from, but he must have done a bunk soon after firing at your van. We are tracking him now across a field of corn that backs onto the tree line. I will give you further information as we get it." The helicopter was searching in a pattern back and forth ahead of the tactical squad, who were advancing through the corn.

"Sergeant, could you come up to where we are, please?"

"Already coming, Captain. Constable, we can stand up now and brush ourselves off, but stay down below the embankment until we get the all-clear from the tac boys."

The constable stood up and looked down at her uniform, which had grass stains and cow dung on the front of it. "Make that thirty minutes in the ring at the gym, Captain. Do you know what the guys are going to say about you and I, especially with me covered in grass seeds, grass stains, and cow dung?"

"Just refer them to me, Constable, as I am sure there would have been some brown-stained pants if some of the men had been driving. You did very well there, Constable. That was some quick thinking on your behalf to work out where the shots were coming from and to put the embankment between the shooter and us. There will be a mention of your actions in the report when I write it."

Chapter 13

THE TACTICAL SQUAD ARRIVES

The sergeant pulled up on the road, and he and the sharp shooter were out in a flash, taking cover behind the embankment.

The sergeant came down to where the Captain and Constable were standing next to the van. "You both OK?"

"Just a little shaken, sergeant."

The sarge walked around to the front of the van, which was a little dinged up from the ride through the saplings, but he was looking at the bullet holes in the front windscreen. He walked around to the passenger side and looked at the exit hole of the bullet.

"Only one hole, Captain, so the other round must still be inside the van. Maybe lodged in the sliding door or it hit a seat frame. That's a job for the forensic team when they get here. Probably a .308 calibre, I would say. If we can find that second bullet, we can start hauling in all the shooters in the district with .308 rifles and find out if they have an alibi for this morning. The shooter was doing well to get two shots in the short time he had available. We are looking for a professional or a gifted amateur."

"Sarge, take some of the detectives and some of the new guys coming up here today, and let's see if we can get them while it is still fresh and before they have a chance to clean the weapon. Look for spent shell casings as well that still have that recent-fired smell. These bastards are getting a bit too cocky for my liking."

The leader of the tactical response team came on the radio. "You there, Captain?"

"Yes, go ahead."

"The shooter had a motorbike stashed in the cornfield on a back country road and has got away. I would say he bolted after firing the two shots through the van, so he is long gone. I will say that he is a professional shooter, as to get two shots through the windshield in the time frame that the van was on the road and the distance, he was firing from tells me this was no first-time shooter."

"Right, sergeant, bring the chopper in and get your people picked up and dropped back to where the forensic crew are working. We will space your people out along the road back to the main road and they can keep an eye out just in case. You might like to get the chopper to fly you around this area a bit so you can familiarise yourself with the terrain and the road network."

"Right, sir, consider it done."

"Well, sergeant, you might like to put the constable on the chopper as well so she can point out the areas of interest around here, then the chopper can go into town and refuel. Have one of the traffic branches pick up the pair of them from the chopper pad so the constable can go home and change out of her muddy uniform. When the forensics are finished with the van, arrange for a tow truck to pull the van back up onto the road and take it to the workshop for a safety inspection. I don't think it is badly damaged, but we need to make sure before getting a new windscreen fitted. Make sure we get forensics to have a look at where he was waiting up the tree to see if he left any evidence, fingerprints, or cigarette butts, etc. I want this bludger, and so does the constable."

The Captain got into one of the squad cars and they turned around and headed back to the farm. The captain's teleconference with the commissioner forgotten in the general confusion that was happening.

The Captain spoke to the driver:

"Pull up at the press rabble and I will bring them up to date. Look at the way they are all across the road." The squad car came to a halt and the captain climbed out.

"Right, a bit of quiet, if you please."

The press knew now not to shout at the captain and to do things in an ordered manner. "Questions, you, young lady."

The captain nominated a reporter who was holding a television microphone.

"Captain, we heard two shots fired. Can you elaborate on what happened down the road, as the road was blocked by a squad car and we could not investigate?"

"All right. The constable and myself in the police van were fired upon by a sharpshooter who was stationed up a tree some distance off the road. Two shots came through the front windscreen and passed between the constable, who was driving, and myself. The quick thinking by the constable driving off the road and down the embankment leading up to the bridge saved us from taking any further incoming fire from the shooter. We have brought in a tactical response team from Sydney who landed near the river and searched the tree line for the assailant. The shooter appears to have fled the scene immediately after firing the two shots. He escaped on foot and then by trail bike; however, we will be keeping the Sydney squad here until such time as we have finished our investigation here on the farm. The forensic people will be examining the van we were travelling in, and it will stay in the field until such time as they have completed their investigation. Nobody from the press is to try and approach the van, as that is considered a crime scene. That is all that I have for you at this time. Thank you."

The captain turned and climbed into the squad car, which blew its horn and started moving forward towards the farm.

The press people moved off the road, but they were all talking amongst themselves and heading for the TV vans.

"Well, that will be all over Australia within five minutes. To the farm, detective, I need a drink of water and something to eat if there is anything left."

Five minutes later, the captain, water bottle in hand, walked across to where the forensic team and the backhoe were working.

"How is it going, people?"

"Not as exciting here, Captain, as what your morning has been. We are almost at the bottom of the rubbish pit. One interesting thing about this rubbish pit is that there is a net made out of wire mesh with a sling on each corner. I could not work out what it was for at first, then it came to me that the slings could be attached to the front-end loader on a tractor, and all the rubbish could be lifted out of the pit in one go. At a later time, it could all be lifted back in, and the slings coiled up and hidden in the rubbish. The only reason I can imagine is that they could bury things below the rubbish and then cover it all over again. I would not be surprised to find more than one cadaver at the bottom of this pit."

"Well, whatever you find, treat it with the respect due to a young life taken early."

"Sergeant."

"Yes, Captain."

"We need to make sure that nobody comes sneaking back into the trees after dark, so we need a team with night-vision gear to keep the area under observation during the night. Have the boys doing a walk-around found anything of interest?"

"Well, they have not had a lot of time available for searching; however, there are a few places that appear low for no apparent reason. The Sydney people should be here soon, so we can start being a bit more methodical about what we are doing. If you look across there, you will see a stake with an orange tape fluttering in the wind. Well, that is one of the low locations."

"If there is a free forensic person and the backhoe comes available, put it to work there excavating."

Chapter 14

EXCAVATING THE RUBBISH PITT

The Captain and the sergeant walked across to the stake.

The captain stopped some distance away.

"Can you feel anything, Sergeant?"

"Not sure what you mean, Captain."

"Evil and sadness, Sergeant."

"No, sir. I am not a very sensitive person, so no, I cannot feel anything."

"Well, Sergeant, you will find another lost soul buried here. Treat this excavation with respect, as there is another victim calling for justice, and I am determined to get the animals who have buried these young people here, where there has been no family to grieve for them."

"Yes, sir."

The Captain turned and walked away back to his car. The sergeant was thinking that the captain was losing his marbles and needed a rest, but it was not his job to question his superior.

Gradually, order returned to the farm with the forensic people excavating the rubbish pit, the tactical squad establishing a perimeter around the farm, and the traffic squad doing a search-and-find exercise around the farmhouse.

The captain walked away and found a seat under a shady tree and had a bite to eat and another bottle of water. He was just settling down when his phone rang again. A quick glance told him it was the Time Walker.

"Hello, young fellow."

"Hello, Captain. I am sorry for what happened this morning. I was working on another time, and when I came back to you, I saw what had happened to you. I have checked the shooter out, and I cannot find anything that will identify him at this time, as he was wearing a balaclava the whole time. I have a difficult time tracking high-speed cars and motorbikes, but I am working on modifying my equipment, and hopefully down the road, I will be able to come back to this scene and help you out. His number plate on the motorbike was obscured, and he was quick and was gone by the time the helicopter arrived."

"That's okay, young fellow. It was a bit exciting there for a few minutes, but nobody was injured. We are still excavating the rubbish tip, but we have found another location that I am sure holds another victim."

"Well, Captain, you have enough on your plate at the moment, so stay safe, and I will keep an eye out over the whole site. Don't forget my rewards, and Captain, take some extra precautions, as these people could try again to put you out of the picture. Goodbye, Captain."

The phone went dead, and the Captain was just sitting down when he got a shout from the forensic people. "Captain. Come here, please, if you would."

The captain walked over to the excavated rubbish pit and looked down and saw exposed bones of a hand.

"Captain, this is now a crime scene as well."

"I want you to treat the remains with reverence because this person has waited twenty or more years for justice. Is that understood?"

"Yes, Captain."

"When you have all the remains removed, excavate a little deeper, as I think you will find another set of bones below this set."

There was silence in the pit as the captain walked away. The techie whispered to his off-sider, "I thought the captain was losing his marbles, but he was spot on about this rubbish pit."

"Have you noticed that he gets a phone call every so often, and then the Captain seems to know more than anyone else?" said the second techie.

"I don't care where he gets his info from because we are finding more burial sites and information than ever before. Let's just keep doing what the Captain asks. I bet there is another body buried under this one, so we had better be spot-on with our forensic work so we don't get shown up in a court of law."

They both went back to exposing the whole skeleton.

Chapter 15

REMOVING THE FIRST FARM VICTIM

It was later in the day when the second forensic group arrived on site after bullying their way through the press people gathered at the gate.

The sergeant met the crew and instructed them to go to where the shooter had been hiding up the tree and see if they could find any fingerprints or other evidence.

Two of the crew were to concentrate on the van and see if they could find the second bullet which did not exit the van like the first round did. Two of you stay here so we can start this other excavation with the backhoe while they finalize the removal of the skeleton from the old rubbish tip. The sergeant called one of his uniformed boys across and spoke to him and the two forensic people. "Constable, get the backhoe and show these forensic people where we have staked what we believe is another grave site and have the backhoe work under their direction."

"Will do, sarge."

The sergeant got into his vehicle and led the rest of the forensic people in their van out of the gate. The press people clustered around the vehicles, all calling out questions which the police ignored.

The chopper had long since come to the farm and headed into town, so the captain looked about and thought about the good times he and the football team had here many years ago.

Parties and barbecues. It seemed like a whole different world now that they were finding the remains of murder victims.

The backhoe moved across to the pegged suspected grave and started setting itself up to begin digging. The captain walked toward the front gate of the farm to stretch his legs and to give the press people a bit more information.

The press people started calling out while he was still 50 meters away. The captain stopped and held his hands up. The press people went silent. He walked the remaining distance to the police car at the gate.

He called one of the traffic police who were stationed at the gate to come over and stand beside him.

"Right, some further information for the press. We have removed all the rubbish from a rubbish pit and excavated underneath where the rubbish had been, and we have found the remains of a skeleton. Forensics are now, with compassion, removing those remains which will be transported to the Sydney forensic labs for analysis and DNA testing."

"Captain, a question."

"Yes. Go ahead."

"We notice that the backhoe has moved to another location and is just now starting to dig. Can you tell us why, please?"

"Well, we have found a depression in the ground which appears suspicious to us, so we are excavating to see if there are any human remains buried there as well. If we find anything, I will let you know. That is all the information that we have for the press at this time. Thank you."

The captain turned and with slumped shoulders walked back toward the farmhouse.

The press was quiet for a few minutes, then they all turned and went back to their TV vans to spread the word about a second set of remains found in this country town in the one week.

The whisper on everyone's lips was serial killer.

The time passed, and the captain saw the forensic people and the sergeant making their way past the news people. A few minutes later, they stopped beside the Captain.

"Well, Captain, you were correct. We found the second bullet in the side sliding door. You are a lucky man, Captain. It actually went through the seat you were sitting on after coming through the front window. We strung some coloured thread from the windscreen through the seat and into the side door and photographed it. This was a deliberate attempt on your life, Captain. The spent bullet was a bit mangled, but the forensic boys say it is a .308 calibre, all right."

"Right, sergeant, pass that on to the detectives in town who are already out looking into all the owners of .308 rifles registered in the district and where they were this morning.

I think we will find that it is a stolen, unregistered weapon."

"Captain, I also have the forensic guys with me who went and checked out where the shooter was sitting up the tree. They have samples of cotton threads from the tree branches, but he must have been wearing gloves as he climbed the tree. He had driven in metal railway spikes to make it easier to climb the tree, but no fingerprints. The guy was very professional."

"Right, sergeant. I want to leave the area in your hands and the forensic people. If you have any questions, give me a call on my mobile."

"Right, Captain. This investigation is getting bigger all the time, Captain."

"Right, I am going back to the office to have that phone conference with the commissioner that I was supposed to have hours ago. I will have a tow truck sent out to pull the van back onto the road and load it onto a tilt tray to take it into the station."

With that, the Captain climbed into the sergeant's car and asked, "A driver, please, sarge, then he can come straight back out here. Open the road up and let the news people go back into town if they so wish."

The sergeant nodded, and the car disappeared up the road and turned into town.

The captain was quiet all the way back to town. Things were happening too quickly for his liking, but he had to act on the tip-offs the Time Walker was giving him.

Chapter 16

WARNING TO THE CAPTAIN

There appeared to be as many newspaper and TV people in town as there were out along the road near the farm. This did not improve the captain's disposition as he went through the back door into his office.

He doubled back and spoke to the staff in the detectives' squad room.

"Right, you all got the information that it was a .308 round that went through the van?"

A chorus of "Yes, sir" echoed around the squad room. "What progress have we made on the investigation to date?"

"Well, Captain, every person with a licensed .308 in the district that we have spoken to has either been at work, where they have other people to vouch for them, or they have been at home watching the cricket and were more than willing to show us their rifle. None had been fired recently, and all ammunition could be accounted for."

"Right, what about ownership of the farm and anyone who had used the farm?"

"Still waiting on the Lands department to send us the list of owners for the last 25 years, Captain."

"The Privacy Act meant we had to get a warrant from the Chief Justice, but we should have it by late afternoon."

"Well, keep at it because we want these buggers as soon as possible. The constable would also like to have one of them in the gym boxing ring for half an hour as well."

"You talking about me, Captain?"

"Yes, constable. You did a great job out there today, and that will be mentioned in my report to the commissioner."

"Thank you, Captain."

"I will be in my office if anybody wants me. Okay?"

A nodding of heads as the captain went into his office.

The detectives turned as one and started to question the constable about what had happened.

Nothing like this had happened in this police district ever before, so it was a source of interest to them all.

The constable kept it short and sweet, which left a lot of the detectives asking for more information.

The constable just turned and went back to her desk out in front of the police station.

The captain dialled the commissioner, and the phone was answered on the first ring.

"Hello, Captain. What have you got for me?"

"Commissioner, another grave site with a possible two more tomorrow. Looks like the farm was used as a torture chamber and then they buried them there. Something must have scared them to make them move to burying them in the national park, or the one in the national park was the first one. How are the lab people going down there with what they have to date? Have they isolated any DNA that we can use?"

"Captain, there has been a lot of work come in from your area, which is creating a bit of a backlog, but we will have it soon. What is a concern now is that we are possibly looking at four grave sites. Where did they all come from?

You only have two missing people in your police district, and you have a big district. Were these people driving long distances to get victims? Some of them could be from Sydney even. We have our share of missing persons going back a long time."

"Captain, I want you to be very aware of your safety from now on. If these people are prepared to try and shoot you and failed, then they might try again closer to home. Is that clear, Captain?"

"Yes, sir. I will take precautions coming and going home from work."

"All right. I don't want any police fatalities. I spoke to the premier this afternoon, and he is arranging for the reward to be paid for the first victim found. We will need to identify all the victims before we can work out just what is owing to your young fellow."

The commissioner hung up, and the captain was left sitting with the phone in his hand, thinking about how they were going to identify all the remains.

The captain stood up, took off his suit coat, and hung it on the chair. He then opened the wardrobe in his office, took out a bulletproof vest, and put it on.

He then went to the safe, opened the combination, and took out his handgun and shoulder holster.

"Been a while since I wore this, but it was like riding a push bike," the captain thought back to all the shooting competitions he had been in.

He had won a lot of trophies when he was younger. Now that he was a lot older, it seemed strange to be dressing for a possible shootout.

He took the Glock 19, opened the breech, and checked the mechanism. He took out a magazine loaded with 19 rounds of 9mm ammunition and slipped the magazine into the butt. Checked all was good to go and slipped the handgun into the holster.

He then donned his suit coat again and checked himself in the full-length mirror on the wall.

No noticeable bulges as he always had his suits cut a little fuller where his handgun nestled.

There was a knock on the door to his office.

"Yes, come in. Good afternoon, constable. That uniform looks a lot cleaner than the one you were wearing this morning. Now, what can I do for you?"

"Captain, just had a phone call from the farm. The location where you put the backhoe to work has found another victim. The forensic people have asked we stop digging for a while until they catch up."

"I will ring the sergeant and talk to him. Thank you for the message."

"Captain, can I say please take extra care, as I don't think these people are finished trying to eliminate you from this investigation."

The captain tapped his chest and said, "Already taking precautions, constable. Thanks for the concern."

The captain dialled the number for the sergeant and waited.

The sergeant came on the line. "Hello, Captain."

"Sergeant, hold off on any further digging until the forensic boys catch up. Please."

"Already stopped, Captain. We are about to knock off for the day, sir."

"That's all right, sergeant. Have the tactical response people set up a perimeter around the farm?"

"Yes, sir, and the chopper will do a flyover first thing in the morning with infrared detection just to make sure we don't have any unwanted guests."

"Thanks for everything, sergeant. It has been a full-on day. I am looking forward to a quiet beer when I get home."

"Yes, sir. See you tomorrow morning."

The captain left the office and went out the rear door of the police station.

He took the gate through the rear fence into the laneway and left the press out in the street in front of the police station.

The captain turned at the next street and headed up towards his house, lost in thought.

Chapter 17

ATTEMPT ON THE CAPTAIN'S LIFE

"Hello, Captain. Things pretty busy at the moment according to the news."

"Yair. Hello, Bob. I think I need to be retired like yourself. Been stressful, mate."

Bob was the captain's next-door neighbour; a retired bank manager whose passion now was his gardens.

There was a squeal of tires on the bitumen, and both Bob and the captain looked up the road at a white SUV accelerating toward them.

"Get down, Bob, this does not look good."

The passenger of the SUV leaned out the window and pointed a handgun at the captain and started firing.

The captain could hear bullets going past him down the road and thudding into the pin oak tree growing on the footpath outside of Bob's house.

The captain took two steps sideways closer to the road to lessen the chance of Bob getting hit by a stray round.

While he was moving, he reached across his body and drew his Glock, and in one smooth movement, he raised his pistol and fired two shots through the passenger side of the front windscreen. A spray of red mist flew away from the shooter across the inside of the car and across the driver. The driver pulled the wheel to the right to escape the stream of blood, then realized his mistake too late and lost control of the SUV, which went careening across the road and clipped a large Japanese maple tree. The SUV then mounted the footpath on the opposite side of the road from where the captain was standing and rammed the concrete fence across the road.

The captain was across the road and heading for the SUV when the driver exited the car and swung a mini-Uzi submachine gun across the roof of the SUV and attempted to fire at the captain.

"Police! Drop the weapon and put your hands in the air."

The driver ignored the call and finally got the safety catch off and swung the weapon toward the captain.

"Look out, Captain!" called Bob.

The captain dropped down onto one knee and fired two shots at the driver, who reeled back.

A burst of machine gun fire blasted leaves off the maple tree as the gun pointed skyward, then went silent.

The captain warily moved back away from the SUV and sidled around the back of the vehicle. The engine was still screaming as one of the drive wheels was in the air.

The captain slowly walked up to the SUV and looked at the driver. One glance was enough to tell that he was no longer a threat, as one bullet had entered through his left eye and the second had lodged in his throat.

He checked the passenger, and he was in a similar condition, with both rounds the captain had fired finding a home in his face.

He went back to the driver's side, leaned in, and, with a tissue taken from his pocket, turned the key of the SUV into the off position.

The silence was deafening.

The scream of sirens and howls of engines split the air as two patrol cars came around the corner. The captain moved to the centre of the road, bent down, placed his pistol on the ground, and held both hands in the air.

He was pleased that his patrolmen were so quick, but he did not want to be shot by accident.

Both cars came to a halt, and four patrolmen spilled out with guns drawn.

"Move away from the gun, keep your hands in the air."

"Guys, it is the Captain. Put your guns down." It was Bob, the next-door neighbour, calling out.

Tension in the air started to lessen as the guns slowly went down.

"Gee, sorry, Captain," said the eldest of the four patrolmen. "But it's getting a bit dark."

"That's all right, men, you are only doing your job."

"What happened, Captain?"

"Seems as though some people really dislike me. Are you okay, Bob?"

"Yes, Captain. When you stepped sideways, the gunfire started to follow you, though there were a few anxious moments there."

"Okay, Corporal, call the detective squad and the forensic people. Barricade the street so we keep the news people out of here for a while." The corporal nodded, and one patrolman went further up the street, and one went down the street just in time to stop the cameramen from running up the street.

The captain handed his pistol to the corporal. "You will need this for a little while, and I don't think there is any more danger to me, as I only have 30 meters to go across to my very nervous wife who is waiting at the gate."

"When the detectives get here, send them across to my place, and we will work out where we go from here."

"Yes, sir."

People were coming out of their houses very slowly, looking about to see what had happened.

The corporal started talking into his radio, and more police cars were coming as the captain turned and went to his wife across the road, waiting at the gate.

"Hello, love. How about a cup of tea with an extra spoon of sugar, please?"

"All right, love, but what is going on in our quiet town?"

"Madness, darling. I have no idea, but there are some evil people who don't like me."

The captain put his arm around his wife and moved back towards his back door.

When she went into the house, he turned and went to the gazebo and sat down.

The street filled with police erecting barricades and ensuring that the crime scene was not disturbed.

The captain took out his phone and dialled the police commissioner in Sydney.

The phone was answered on the second ring.

"Hello, Captain. What can I do for you?"

"Well, commissioner, there has been an attempted drive-by shooting; however, that was foiled, and the two gang-banger shooters are unfortunately dead. They were shot and killed in the shootout. Nobody else was injured—more by good luck than anything, as they had automatic weapons."

"Bloody hell, Captain, who or what was the target?"

"I was the target, commissioner, and I am the person who shot both of them. The attempt was just outside my house."

"Bloody hell, Captain, you have really stirred up a hornet's nest. I will get some more tactical squad people up there tonight. I want you and your wife with bodyguards 24 hours a day until this whole case is finished. I am also sending up the chief forensic officer and a lot more equipment. What is the body count now, Captain?"

"Three, sir, but the possibility of more when the forensic people catch up with what they are doing now. We could find a few more victims out on that farm."

"OK. Keep me informed, and I have had the young fellow's reward approved. Now we need to work out how he gets paid and where."

"Yes, sir. Good evening."

The captain rang off, and his phone rang almost immediately.

"Hello, young fellow. How are you?"

"More to the point, Captain, how are you?"

"Not a scratch."

"Well, I did warn you. I cannot see the future, only the past. I have had a look at what happened, and you did very well to stop them from shooting you. A lot of practice when you were younger has paid off."

"The commissioner has told me that he has got your reward approved. Now you need to let me know how and where you want the money sent to."

"Thank you, Captain. I knew you were an honest man and a man of principles, which is why I chose you. Now, when you have finished out at the farm, I will send you another memory stick, and this will show you some horrific things and the evil people who did them.

I will get back to you with my banking details. Take care, Captain."

The line went dead.

The captain's wife arrived with a teapot of tea, some mugs, and some freshly made muffins. They both sat down in the gazebo.

The police sergeant and a detective came through the yard gate and walked down to the captain. The captain and his wife both stood up.

"Sit down, sergeant, detective, and pour yourself a mug of tea. Make sure you put in an extra spoonful of sugar. It has been a wild day, and I hope I don't have any more of them. Did the corporal hand my pistol in to the forensic people?"

The four of them sat down for a moment, poured a mug of tea, and had a muffin.

Silence reigned for a bit in the gazebo, then the sergeant spoke.

"Thank you, Captain. Now would you please stand up for a moment?"

"Of course, sergeant, but please tell me why I am standing up?"

The sergeant leaned over, took hold of the captain's suit coat, and put his finger through three bullet holes in the coat.

"This is cutting it a bit close, Captain. And there are some on the other side of your body as well. Forensic will want this jacket, so please empty out your pockets for me, please."

Chapter 18

BULLET HOLES FROM A NEAR MISS

The Captain slipped the jacket off and looked at three holes on his left side and one hole on the right side of the jacket.

The captain's wife went faint.

"I have to sit down, dear."

The captain made room for her at the table.

The captain went through his pockets and emptied out some tissues, a face mask, and his wallet and ID badge. He then handed them over to the sergeant for delivery to the forensic people.

"Well, sergeant, if I had not stepped out onto the roadway, then Bob, my next-door neighbour, would have been in the line of fire as well. They would have just stopped the car and shot at both of us, just standing there like a couple of targets. These automatic UZI submachine guns are not very accurate over any great distance. Still, I don't want to be doing this sort of thing every afternoon after work. The commissioner is sending up some more tactical police and wants the wife and me guarded twenty-four hours a day until this whole case is closed off and we have the culprits behind bars."

"That's good news, Captain. My boys are getting stretched out, and the local hoons know that they are not around and are doing burnouts in the main street now. They are in for a shock tomorrow."

"Well, sergeant, detective, you have the jacket. I don't think my tailor can invisibly mend that, and it will be needed at the inquest. I will leave everything to your guys and your people. The bodies will need to be fingerprinted and then taken to the morgue."

"Everything is underway, Captain. We are taking a statement from your next-door neighbour, and while you are finishing your tea, the constable will come and take your statement of events. Then you can go and have a quiet dinner. We will keep an eye on the place until we can get some tactical response people here to guard the scene and your house."

"Thank you, Sarge. Send the constable as soon as she is available. I will sit here with my wife and finish my tea. Please take the muffins out to share with the boys on the street."

"Thank you, Captain."

Chapter 19

BODYGUARD FOR THE CAPTAIN

The Captain and his wife were left alone in the gazebo. The street was a hive of activity—between forensic people digging spent rounds out of trees, cameras taking photos, and tape measures checking the distances of spent cartridge cases to the vehicle.

The captain sat down and had some sweet tea. He could feel the effects of mild shock coming on, so he wanted to get something sweet into his system. He looked up and saw the constable come through the garden gate.

"Good evening, Captain, Mrs. Wilson. Is this a good time to take your statement, Captain?"

"Come in, Constable. Better off getting it now while it's still fresh in my mind."

The constable took out a statement pad and proceeded to record everything that the captain said over the next 20 minutes.

When she was finished, she read it all back to him. He made a couple of minor corrections and then signed it where she indicated.

She closed the pad and looked up at the Captain. "You are a very lucky man, Captain, and a very good shot. Twice in one day is pushing the odds."

"Well, years of shooting competitions made me a good shot, and the young hoodlums using UZI machine pistols gave me an advantage when it came to a shootout. Using a machine pistol does not make up for a lack of practice at the pistol range."

"Well, I will leave you and your wife to some peace and quiet, Captain. Try and get a good night's sleep. We have plenty to do tomorrow, so a sleep-in would not be considered lazy, especially as tomorrow is Saturday."

The constable made her way out of the yard.

"Love, what did she mean, 'twice in one day'?"

The captain spoke to his wife. "Well, darling, some shooter had a couple of shots at the constable and me as we were driving back to town this morning. He got away, though, and thanks to the constable's driving, he didn't get a chance to take any more shots. Come on, love, time to go into the house. It's getting dark. This mess outside is in good hands, and the boys all know what they're doing."

The captain's wife was in a minor state of shock.

When they were in the house, the captain went into the spare bedroom and opened his gun safe. He took out his personal pistol, found a spare magazine, checked the loads, and slipped it into his harness. He then got a casual jacket and put it on over his bulletproof jacket and gun harness. He wanted to be armed until the tactical response people arrived.

His wife was busy in the kitchen, so he left her alone.

The captain sat down in his recliner rocker and thought about the events of the day.

Time to have a roundtable meeting with all the detectives in the morning and bring the whiteboard up to date.

His wife called, and he went into the dining room, where he found a nice roast lamb with roast vegetables, gravy, and a Yorkshire pudding on the side waiting for him.

"Beautiful, darling. Now sit down yourself, and let's have a quiet meal, even though there's a lot of noise from generators and cars coming and going outside."

They were just finishing the sticky date pudding when the captain heard a chopper going overhead and landing on the helipad in the park.

"That was a great meal, darling. Now I will be sitting on the patio if you need me."

The captain made his way to the side patio and sat down, watching the forensic people finishing up their work.

The bodies were long gone to the morgue, and there was a tilt-tray truck loading the damaged SUV onto the tray to be taken to the police impound yard.

Things were starting to come back to normal when a police vehicle stopped outside the captain's house.

The sergeant got out along with two tactical response officers and headed to the captain's front gate.

"Over here, Sergeant."

"Good evening, Captain. These are the two tactical response officers who are here for the night. One of them will stay here in the morning, and the other one will escort you to the station in the morning if you wish to go there."

"Sergeant, I want a meeting with all the staff first thing in the morning before they head out to the farm or hit the streets. That includes the forensic and tactical response people, plus the chopper pilots. I want you and your traffic boys there as well. It will be a quick meeting so the night-shift people can get away for a rest as soon as possible. Is 7 a.m. too late?"

"No, Captain. I'll pass the word to everyone."

"Sergeant, you get away now and have a rest as well."

"Aye, aye, Captain."

The sergeant headed off just as the tilt-tray truck disappeared down the road. The street was now almost back to normal, with some curious neighbours still hanging about the place in small groups.

The captain stood up and gestured to the two tactical response officers, who were well-armed with automatic weapons and handguns.

"Come and meet the wife."

They followed the captain through into the kitchen from the side patio.

"Darling, we have some guests who will be staying here for a few days."

The captain's wife turned and was surprised to confront the two tactical officers in her kitchen.

"Right, people, there's a very comfortable couch out there on the patio, so one of you can grab a kip while the other is up and about. There's a fridge there with some sliced bread, cold lamb, mint sauce, and cold vegetables, so you can help yourself. There's a kettle on top of the fridge with coffee, tea, milk, and sugar, so help yourself. I don't expect any more issues from anyone at this time. Thank you for being here. By the way, there's a toilet and hand basin behind that door."

The pair just nodded their heads and turned back out to the patio, where they were discussing what they were going to do for the night around the house.

The captain's wife was shaking her head. "Our quiet street has been turned into a circus, and you nearly got yourself shot twice in one day. Australia is getting to be just like America. I hope you can get this whole business sorted out soon, love. I'm going off to bed and trying to forget what has happened today."

"I'll be in for a shower in a minute, love. I just want to catch the news."

The captain turned on the TV and settled into his recliner to watch the news.

Naturally, the news was all about the shooting in the morning and the shooting in the afternoon. There was a lot of speculation, guessing, and fiction when they didn't know the truth.

The captain went for a shower and then settled in for a night's sleep.

It was 5 a.m., and the captain was up, showered, and dressed. He had on a good pair of R.M. Williams jeans and a long-sleeved shirt. He donned the bulletproof vest, the shoulder holster, and added a zip-up waterproof jacket. He checked in the mirror that the gun holster was not visible.

He went to the kitchen and started cooking some bacon and eggs.

He put his head out the door and spoke to the two tactical response officers. "No vegans here, is there?"

Both heads shook negatively. "Bacon and eggs, toast, and coffee?"

Two heads nodded in the affirmative.

"Right, come in and sit down. Coffee is ready, toast is done. There's some butter in the fridge, grab it please. Two eggs each and bacon to keep you going. How was your night?"

Both officers nodded and mumbled, "Good, sir." Neither officer had ever had a captain make them breakfast before.

Soon, the three of them were eating breakfast and enjoying a cup of coffee.

"Right, one of you will need to stay here with the wife, and the other come with me to the station when we've finished breakfast. Plenty of time before our meeting at 7 a.m."

The captain's wife came into the kitchen wearing a bathrobe over her nightdress. "Good morning, all. I see you're going to the station this morning, darling."

More a statement than a question.

"Yes. We need to have a meeting this morning to find out just where we are in the investigation. The activities of yesterday meant that everything else was overlooked, so this morning is catch-up time."

When the three police officers had finished, they stood up, and both tactical officers thanked the captain for breakfast. They both went outside and had a good look around.

"Darling, one of the squad will stay here today with you. The officer will be changed out after our meeting. We're off now to the station. I should be home by lunchtime."

The captain and one officer headed out when the officer gave the nod to do so.

A police car had just done a patrol up the street and around the corner to check if there were any cars loitering about the place.

"Stay very close behind me, Captain. I understand that you are a very good shot, but let's not get involved in any shootouts this morning."

Chapter 20

ANOTHER PRESS CONFERENCE

They set a quick pace down to the back gate of the station, where they were met with two more tactical squad people. "Straight into the station, Captain. No mucking about. This is a very vulnerable location here until we can clear all the buildings that front the carpark."

Within a half minute, they were inside the police station. The captain was pleased to see a one hundred percent turnout and not yet six-fifteen.

"Good morning, all."

There was a rousing "Good morning, Captain" from everyone.

"Right, people, first I want to say a big thank you to everyone here for the big effort yesterday. Not your normal day by any means. Now we need to first bring me up to date on our investigation. Forensic?"

"Captain, the lab in Sydney has been able to get a sample that they can check for DNA, but it will be a week or so before we can accurately say who was in the first grave in the national park. We have exhumed the remains from the rubbish pit, and they have been sent to the lab in Sydney last evening. Today, we will start exhuming the remains from the second excavation we have found at the farm. Now that we have additional colleagues from Sydney, we will excavate further in the rubbish pit and see if your hunch about another victim below the first victim is correct. We have not received any information back yet on the axe handles. The shooting yesterday morning and last evening has meant a lot more work preparing everything for the coroner for the double fatality. That's about it, Captain."

"Right, my apologies for the additional work caused by the shootings last evening. However, I was not given a lot of choice in the matter."

"Right, Sergeant, your boys have done a whole lot of extra work over the last couple of days, and it is good to see that you have extra people here to assist you in their duties. I will leave you to work with the tactical response people in getting to know where everything is until we have things back to normal. Again, thank you, guys and ladies, you have all been a great help. Tactical response people, it is very good to see you here. When people start shooting at us, we are moving out of the area of normal police training. Please split your people up into their areas of responsibility, and if I or the sergeant can assist in any way, then please do not hesitate to call for us."

Lastly, but not least, we have our chopper personnel, who we much appreciated yesterday when you swooped in and dropped off the tactical response people. I understand one chopper will be staying here to assist with infrared passes over the farm each day to ensure that no unwanted people have made their way back to have another shot at the constable and myself."

"Are there any questions?"

"No. All right. Chief Detective, I see that our squad of news people have increased in numbers outside. I don't want to expose myself or anyone else out there for any length of time at this time, so could you select six newspaper and six TV people to come into our training room, and I will bring them up to date. Now, people, no heroics and stay safe out there."

The squad room started emptying. The Captain called to the Constable, who had been in the van with him the day before. "Go into the training room and draw all the blinds and make sure the lights are on and the AC is working. Chief Detective, when you go outside, ensure that the people you select really are newspaper people and not locals who want some of the news first-hand. Take a couple of Tach squad with you and don't take any rubbish from them."

"Yes, Sir."

The Captain went into the training room and turned on the urn. He checked that there were enough paper mugs, milk, and sugar. He had found over the years that if you gave them a coffee early in the morning, they were usually a little less like wolves.

There was a howl outside when the fifth estate realised that not all of them were going to be allowed inside. Finally, after fifteen minutes, they started to filter into the training room.

When they were all inside, the Captain invited them to sit down, get a coffee if you want one, and then I will bring you up to date on the progress of our investigation.

Finally, there was quiet in the training room, and the Chief Detective and the Constable were seated alongside the Captain.

"Right, people, you are aware that yesterday the Constable here and myself were the subject of a shooter firing two rounds from a long rifle through the police van. We were very lucky as the rounds passed through the seat alongside where I was sitting. Only quick thinking on the behalf of the Constable, who was driving, to get the vehicle off the road and hidden behind the road embankment; otherwise, there could have been more rounds fired into the van.

The forensic people have discovered two grave sites on the farm in question. We will continue to look for more graves before we say that there are no more bodies buried there.

We have stationed here now two squads of tactical police and a helicopter to move them about if needed.

Now, to the events of last evening, I was on my way home after work, and I stopped on the footpath next to my neighbour's place for a chat when a white SUV came down the street under power.

I was able to see that the passenger was leaning out the window and was aiming a submachine gun towards me. He commenced firing at me, and I returned fire from my handgun. This was a purely defensive measure because I and my neighbour were exposed on the street. I hit the passenger, and the driver lost control of the SUV and mounted the footpath on the other side of the road. The driver then exited the vehicle and tried to fire a submachine pistol at me. I called on him that this was the police and to drop the weapon. He disobeyed the order and was about to fire at me when I fired two shots at him. He fired a long burst of fire upwards into the tree as he fell to the ground.

Sadly, both driver and passenger were killed in the exchange of fire. We are currently working on identifying who they both were so we can notify their next of kin. The vehicle was stolen the night before in South West Sydney.

Our forensic teams are still working at the farm, and the tactical response teams will protect them until such time as they are no longer needed. Now, are there any questions?"

Hands went up everywhere.

"Ok, you first."

"Captain, is it true you have found the murder weapons that killed the victims that you have found?"

"We have found some heavy objects that are still being tested by forensics at this time. I will not say anything further at this time on that subject."

"Next question?"

"In the shooting yesterday, is it true that both victims were shot in the head?"

"That is correct, as that was the only area of the shooters that I could see. It was shoot them there or die myself. Let me say that I regret having to shoot them; however, when you are facing two people with Uzi submachine guns intent on shooting you, then you have to make an instant decision whether to shoot them or die yourself, and I don't wish to die at this time. Thank you."

"Why did they want to shoot you, Captain?"

"If I knew that, I could probably have prevented the incident in the first place, but I am not a mind reader."

"Ok, one more question."

"Captain, is it correct that you are getting tip-offs from an unknown source regarding the buried persons on the farm?"

"I don't want to comment on that subject at this time. Thank you, people. Please leave the training room in a tidy state with your used coffee cups in the rubbish bin."

The Captain stood up and left the room after whispering to his staff to ensure that all of them left the station and did not go roaming about.

The Captain made his way back to his staff room and made himself a cup of tea. He then went to his office and sat down to enjoy a cup of tea in a bit of peace and quiet.

Chapter 21

THE CRACK HOUSE

His phone rang.

Looking at the caller ID, he muttered, "Bloody hell, what does the young fellow want now on a Saturday morning?"

"Good morning, young fellow."

"Sorry to disturb your peace and quiet, Captain, but I have been trying to work out why somebody wants you dead. The bodies have been there for twenty-plus years, and now you are singled out for revenge. I finally cracked it early this morning. That's a pun, Captain. It's the crack house across the road from the farm. If you send somebody out to the letterbox outside, you will find another memory stick which has my bank details and a video of the farmhouse across the road from the farm where the bodies are. You have some tactical response people here in town, which you will need, as the people in there are very well-armed. Only apply for a warrant when you have everything planned out and your people in position, as there is an informer in the courthouse who will phone them if any warrants are applied for. Check out the young person on the front desk who has a number in her phone under C for Crack. Have a good day, Captain."

The phone went dead.

"My tea has gone cold again."

"Constable Wilkins?"

"Yes, Captain. You bellowed?"

"Sorry, but my day started so well, and now it is going downhill again. Would you be so good as to check our letterbox for another memory stick and please see if there is one of the tactical response leaders still in the office? Thank you."

The constable was back in a minute with an envelope, which she handed to the Captain.

"Your friend again?"

"Yes, now we need the tactical officer so we can plan a raid. Wait a moment, is our IT person in the station?"

"Yes, Captain."

The Captain handed the memory stick over to the constable. "You know what to do with this and hang about and make sure that he does not make any copies. We still have a leak here in the station."

"Aye, aye, Captain."

Five minutes later, the constable and the tactical response leader were back in the Captain's office.

"Is the sergeant in the station?"

"No, sir, he has left for the farm."

"Thank you."

"You wanted me, Captain?"

"Sit down here next to me and watch this video. What you are about to see is for your eyes only."

The memory stick went into the Captain's desktop and it showed a drone view of the farm where they were excavating for the buried victims. Then it moved across and down the road about fifty meters to the entrance of another farm on the other side of the road. The drone then climbed up to a few hundred feet to give an aerial view across the farmhouse and surroundings. It covered all the area around the farmhouse out to three hundred yards, then moved back to the farmhouse and down into one of the sheds where there were a number of people in white lab coats working on various apparatus and then through to a weighing room and bagging room. The view then went across to the farmhouse where there were people sleeping and where there was a large mound of small plastic bags on a large table waiting for pickup.

The tactical officer spoke first. "How did you get this video, Captain? If this is real, then this is a major drug source for Sydney drug dealers."

"Firstly, the video is real. I have no doubt about that. Secondly, we need to plan a raid after observation to see if we can also catch the pickup vehicles. That way we can track them to their delivery point in Sydney. The problem is, the more people who know about this, the more chance of a leak to the criminals or the press."

"You are right there, Captain. Let me study this some more and we will work out a plan. We will get some vehicle trackers and attach them to any vehicles that go into the farm."

"Well, they must be coming at night time, as there has been no traffic during the day since we started working on the farm. Let's grab a vehicle and go check on progress at the farm."

"Give me a couple of minutes, Captain. I will give you a call when I have a vehicle. Finish off your tea."

"Cold tea again," muttered the Captain. "Suppose I need to ring the commissioner regarding this new development and the young fellow's bank details."

The commissioner answered the phone before the third ring.

"Hello, Captain. How can I help you?"

"Well, Commissioner, some further developments from my young friend. He surmises that the attempts on my person are all about the farmhouse across the road from the farm where we are exhuming bodies being a drug manufacturing factory. I have the two tactical response teams here. Should we raid the place immediately or wait and watch?"

"Captain, we have known for some time that there are drugs coming into Sydney from out your way. We know where they are going to and who is transporting them, but until now, we have not known where they were being manufactured. We have tried tracking them, but they always drop off the radar when they get over the Blue Mountains. They start using back country roads to stay away from the cameras along the main roads. They also swap vans and number plates. How long before you are ready to raid so we can coordinate raids around the storage places here in Sydney?"

"Commissioner, I will leave the details to the tactical response teams to coordinate the raid in line with your tactical response people in Sydney. They are the experts in these matters. I will just go along for the ride."

"Good thinking, Captain. Just shut them down."

"Commissioner, I will send the young fellow's bank details down to you by email later today. You might shake up the labs down there doing the DNA testing, as there are at least three more remains of victims coming down to Sydney in the next few days. I am sure some of those remains will have a reward offered for their recovery, and the young fellow will ask for the rewards after we have identified them."

"Well, Captain, he has been most helpful, so he is entitled to the rewards, especially if he helps us nail the guilty parties."

The Captain found that the commissioner had hung up again. The Captain shook his head and muttered to himself.

Chapter 22

PLANNING THE RAID

The constable and the tactical response officer were at the door of his office. "Got a vehicle, Captain."

"Right, let's get out of here before the ghouls outside see me."

Forty minutes later, the Captain and his entourage arrived at the farmhouse where the forensic people were working. It was a real hive of activity, with the backhoe back at work digging at the old rubbish dump.

They exited the vehicle, and all three looked across the road at the farmhouse suspected of being the drug manufacturing centre. It was a typical farmhouse with outbuildings set back about three hundred meters from the rural road.

"Captain, are you sure that this is for real?"

The constable spoke before the captain could say anything.

"The information that the captain has been given will be one hundred percent accurate. Our informant has never been wrong yet."

"Well, what does this informant look like, and what does he do?"

The constable spoke first.

"I am the only one to have seen him, and I have never seen his face. We don't know his name or where he comes from, but he has never let the Captain down yet."

"OK, just curious, is all. I will get our drone working tonight when it is dark, and we will use some infrared to find out how many people we have there and where they are staying. I will catch up with the other tactical response team, and we will plan a raid based on the numbers, and we've been warned that they are well-armed. I will also liaise with my boss in Sydney so we can coordinate everything to get as many of the dealers and the big boys as possible."

The Captain replied, "It is up to you people, but I also want the snitch in the courthouse, so we raid them at the same time. Now, I want to see how we are going finding the people buried here."

The Captain and the constable walked across to the rubbish dump and spoke to the leader of the forensic team.

"How are we going, people?"

"Slowly, Captain. Your little shootout and your run-in with a sniper have set us back a day or so."

"Have you found any more likely burial places?"

"Captain, when we have sorted out these burial places, we will get the ground-penetrating radar out and have a look-see at some other locations, but let us finish off these two locations first."

"Just asking, guys. They have been resting here a long time, so let's do this right so we can get the mongrels who buried them here. You are all doing a great job, and I am thankful for your dedication."

The Captain turned and went back to the vehicle.

"Constable, grab the tactical response officer, and we will go back to town and leave the professionals here to do their work in peace without me looking over their shoulder all the time."

The three police piled into the car and headed back to the office.

The Captain settled into his office when they arrived back at the police station. He dug out the information for the Time Walker's bank details and drafted an email to the Commissioner, giving him the Swiss bank account number and the name he had been given.

He would have the boys see if they could find anybody with that name on any of the electoral rolls; however, he doubted that they would be so lucky, or the Time Walker would be so naive as to use his own name.

If he could look back in time, he would have bank accounts around the world, and the moment the reward hit his Swiss bank account, it would be transferred to the Bahamas or the Channel Islands or some other banking country that did not give away information easily to other governments.

The Captain decided to call it a day and head home.

He got his escort, and they headed out the back door. The tactical response officer confirmed that they had checked out all the buildings that overlooked the police station and cleared them all, having them under observation so no sniper could use them.

The Captain's street was back to its usual calm and quiet when he arrived home. Bob, his neighbour, was working in his garden, and the rest of the street was as if nothing had happened the afternoon before.

Chapter 23

THE SNITCH

Monday dawned bright and sunny, and the Captain settled down with his two bodyguards and had scrambled eggs, bacon, and toast. Then he stood up, and he and his bodyguard headed off to the office.

Both of them never stopped looking left and right, and it was a relief when they were safe and sound inside the police station.

A cup of tea and a shortbread biscuit, and the Captain seated himself in the office.

Nothing ever goes quietly when you are the boss man on a Monday morning.

The tactical response officer knocked on the Captain's office door.

"Do you have a moment, Captain?"

"Come on in. What have you got for me? Better call in the sergeant, the chief of detectives, and Constable Wilkens as well. We need a female for the arrest of the female at the courthouse."

A couple of minutes later, and they were all in the Captain's office.

"Take a seat. We are about to bring everyone up to speed on the farmhouse across the road from the farm where we are working. If you are not aware, it is a crack manufacturing facility, and we are going to get our tactical response people to raid the place and shut it down. Over to you, officer."

"OK, Captain, we did a drone flyover last evening, and what we have is a guard front and back of the farmhouse armed with UZI submachine pistols. There doesn't appear to be any other armed guards, but that does not mean that anyone inside can't pick up arms and return fire. Everyone appears to be inside the house by seven PM.

We will have snipers locked in on the two guards. The chopper will come in over the farmhouse at three hundred feet and call on them all to lay down their weapons and come out of the farmhouse with their hands above their heads. He will light up the whole area with his searchlights but be high enough that the UZI won't have the range to affect the chopper.

If the armed guards fire at the chopper, the snipers will take them out. At that time, the tactical team will move in from the road in their armoured vehicle. The chopper will repeat the warning and tell them that we will use tear gas and force if they do not comply with the warning. If nobody comes out, we go to the next step.

Our men will go in, break down the door, and lob in flashbangs and more tear gas.

If they break out of the house through the rear, the chopper will be able to direct us using infrared and a searchlight after we have secured the buildings.

We will need the sergeant to block off the main road so wc don't have any vehicular traffic along the road while the operation is underway.

I would also like additional vehicles and officers just in case any drug carrier vans turn up while this operation is underway.

Captain, we need you to get the search warrant so we are all legal. Any questions?"

"What time are we going in, Officer?"

"Seven PM this evening. We will bring all our people into the farm where the forensic people are working during the day, so it looks like part of that operation.

If the sergeant can move the newshounds off the main road and back over the bridge so they are out of range of any stray shots, and the forensic people can all be gone back to town by six-thirty, that would also be good so we have a clear field and no chance of anyone being injured. We need to block off the road both ways so there are no local people driving to town along the road as well. Right, do you all remember the Waco compound in the USA and David Koresh and the 90-odd days of standoff and then the firebombing of the buildings and over 80 dead?"

"I don't want a repeat of that at the farmhouse, so I want two ambulances and a fire truck standing by back behind the bridge over the river. No lights or sirens. Sergeant, can you arrange that, please? I don't want any surprises, as they might try and burn the evidence."

The Captain nodded his agreement to the suggestion.

"Right, Chief Detective, you and I will go up to the courthouse and see the magistrate and, at the same time, grab this snitch who rings any information through to the crack house. We will also need Constable Wilkens in case she goes into the toilet to ring them. No questions?"

Everybody shook their heads.

"Let me make a quick call to the Commissioner and let him know what we are doing."

The phone only rang twice, and the Commissioner was on the phone.

"Yes, Captain, what's happening?"

"Commissioner, we will send in the troops to take the crack house at seven PM this evening."

"Right. I am not happy with just the troops you have there, so I will send a second chopper with infrared equipment and another tactical response team to you within the hour. If need be, they can be on standby, but I want you to have all the manpower you need in case there are any surprises. Best of luck, and everyone stay safe."

"Thank you, Commissioner."

The phone went dead.

"Right, you all heard, so let's get moving as there is a lot to do. Any problems, ring me immediately."

The Captain took out his phone and rang his mate, the magistrate.

The phone rang a couple of times before it was answered.

"Hello, Captain. Looking for another search warrant?"

"Actually, Justice Williams, that is why I have rung you."

"I was just kidding, Captain, but come on up and give me the drum on what you are looking for."

"Justice, there is one other thing, and that is one of your staff is on the payroll of a criminal gang, and we want to nail them at the same time so they don't send out any messages to the gang."

"Bloody hell, Captain, why don't you make my day? Come on up as soon as possible."

"Right, I will be there in about 20 minutes and bring you up to speed about what is happening so you are fully aware that you are in for a busy time over the next week."

The Captain rang off.

"Right, let's head up to the courthouse. When we get there, you two just wait outside while I set things up with the magistrate. When you see the snitch, head for the toilet, follow them in, and get them in the act of phoning, but don't let any message go through and get their phone as well. Could be more than one, so be ready. I want this done quietly so nobody is aware of what happened. All good?"

Two heads nodded, so they headed out to the car park into the waiting car.

The tactical bodyguard climbed in as well, and they pushed their way through the waiting newspaper people.

Nothing was said as they parked outside the courthouse. The four officers went up the stairs and pushed the door open. All heads in the public area turned to look as the armed tactical officer walked in first, followed by the Captain.

Justice Williams was waiting and called, "Come on through, Captain."

The three officers took up a position where they could see everyone in the courthouse office.

The Captain followed his mate, Justice Williams, into his office.

"Take a seat, Bill, and liven up my dull life a bit."

The Captain proceeded to bring the Justice up to speed about where they were with the exhumed bodies and the crack factory that they wanted to raid.

"How did you get information on this crack house, Bill, and has this got something related to the shooting you were involved in the other night outside your house?"

"Well, Justice, we got a tip-off regarding the crack house, and we have done some flyovers with a drone. They are guarding the place with UZI submachine pistols. The farmhouse is right across from the farm where we are exhuming the remains of missing persons. We are assuming that they wanted us to leave before we found out about their little manufacturing facility."

"Now tell me about the person who is on their payroll."

"Well, Justice, when you have made out the warrant, send it out to the front counter to be stamped, and we are certain the guilty person will stamp the warrant and then head for the toilet to get some privacy to phone the crack house. Then we can nail them while they are on the phone, which gives us a little more evidence against them."

"Captain, I am devastated that one of the people here in the justice system is a suspect in this crime. However, money can corrupt anyone. They all sign a declaration that they will not reveal any information about legal matters that come across their desk."

The warrant duly went out to the front desk for witnessing and stamping. The Captain and the Justice walked out front, talking quietly, and after the Captain was handed the warrant, the office girl excused herself and went to the toilet. As soon as she turned the corner, the Captain gave the constable and the detective the nod, and they followed her to the restroom. The constable waited 15 seconds and then went in, finding the office girl with the phone in her hand.

The constable leaned over, took the phone off her, and punched the stop button.

The office girl went to complain until she saw the look on the constable's face.

"Your friends nearly killed the Captain and me, so keep quiet. Detective, come in, please. Keep an eye on our friend while I check out her phone memory."

That only took a few seconds. "Well, what we suspected is correct. Our friend here is part of the drug gang. Now, you can work with us or go down for attempted murder, which will be a long sentence inside. Do you understand?"

The clerk was sobbing. "They said it was only just to let them know, and nobody would ever know, and I needed the money."

"Handcuff her and take her out to the car?"

"No, the Captain wants it done quietly, so nothing gets back to the gang."

"Do you understand, young lady? Walk out with us like we are old friends and come with us to the station for an interview. Do you understand?"

She nodded her head.

"Right, clean up your makeup, and let's all go for a little drive. OK?"

Chapter 24

THE WEAPONS DISCLOSURE

A few minutes later, the detective and the constable, with the young female suspect between them, walked back into the courthouse. While she was not in handcuffs, everyone surmised that she had been arrested.

The Captain spoke quietly to the magistrate. "Mate, spread a story for me that she is being helpful in a stealing and assault case so people don't start talking drugs before we raid the place tonight."

"No worries, Captain, but you take care. I have been hearing stories about your shootout from the town rumour mill, so we will catch up for a quiet ale in the near future, and you can bring me up to date on what is happening about the place."

The Captain shook the magistrate's hand and nodded, then turned and followed the officers, led by the tactical response officer, out to the police vehicle. They headed back to the police station and drove into the backyard. The car parked, and the tactical response officer climbed out and had a good look around before nodding. They all climbed out.

"Put her in a cell till I decide what we are going to do with her, then all of you come to my office."

Once again, the Captain made a cup of tea and headed for his office. He had just sat down when his phone rang again.

"Every time I make a cup of tea; my mate rings me."

"Good morning, young fellow. You have ruined my cup of tea again. What can I do for you now?"

"More like what I can do for you, Captain. I have been having a look at the farmhouse that you are going to raid and have found some very disquieting information. They have more than a few Uzi submachine pistols. They also have a heavy machine gun and at least one RPG (rocket-propelled grenade), and there appear to be about six paramilitary types who look after the security of the place. The manufacturing is all done in the outbuilding, but everyone comes into the farmhouse for meals and to sleep. I think that you need to have a talk with your tactical response officers and allow for more than just a few people with pistols.

They received a phone call last night and are now aware that the police are onto their manufacturing factory. The police have a leak from the Sydney office, which I am trying to trace for you now."

"My cup of tea has gone cold again. Thank you for the call. Please check your Swiss bank account and see if the first instalment has been deposited as I have been told."

"Already, Captain, and it has been transferred to a new account elsewhere. I have just chucked in this crack house as a gesture of good faith. By the way, I will give you a name soon of a rapist who you might like to DNA test now for a cold case from years ago. Bye for now, Captain."

Then he was gone again.

The Captain bellowed, "Constable Wilkens!"

The officer was there in a flash.

"Yes, Captain."

"Get hold of the tactical response leader, the sergeant, and the head of detectives. I need to speak to them urgently. They are a lot better armed out at the farm than we suspected, and there are more of them ready to take up arms. Also, they have been warned we are coming by a leak from Sydney. Get me the IT person as well so we can trace the number in Sydney."

"The Time Walker again?"

The Captain nodded.

"On my way, Captain."

Chapter 25

TENSION BEFORE THE RAID

"Bloody cold tea again," mumbled the Captain. Better call the Commissioner, he thought as he punched in his number.

"Hello, Captain. What is happening?" were the first words from the Commissioner.

"Well, Commissioner, I have been informed that there are about six paramilitary types at the farmhouse, along with a heavy machine gun and at least one RPG. I am trying to get hold of the tactical response leader at this time to bring him up to date on the information."

"Your young friend giving you information again, Captain?" This was said with a slight hint of sarcasm.

"Yes, sir, and every bit of information he has given me has been correct. By the way, you have a security leak in the Sydney office who has notified the crims in the crack house that we are coming."

That shut the Commissioner up, as there was silence for a few moments. "Any idea who we are talking about, Captain?"

"Not yet, sir, but we are tracing every phone call to and from the farm while I speak to you. We'll find the little snitch, just like we found the snitch in the courthouse."

"Captain, when your tactical response leader has decided on their course of action, I will personally handle any further assistance. This way, we will try and keep the snitch out of the loop. When you find out where the leak is, let me know, and I will personally arrest the person myself."

"Thank you, Commissioner. I have to go, as I have the tactical response leader and my people at my door now."

Both phones went dead.

The Captain waved them all into the office and commenced bringing them up to date on the new developments.

The tactical response leader mused, "Well, that puts the raid into a new light. With the two squads we have equipped with automatic weapons, we will target the heavy machine gun first. I will direct the operation from the armoured personnel vehicle, and at any sign of an RPG targeting our vehicle, we will concentrate fire on that window or door. All our people will have night vision equipment and gas masks. Believe me, Captain, my people have trained for this sort of eventuality week after week.

"We will use all of our people concentrated on the front of the house. There will be two sniper teams covering the team. We will fire flashbangs and tear gas into the house from the very start so they will be disoriented before we even leave the shelter of the armoured vehicle. If they escape out the back of the house, we will have a sniper team watching every door and window. The helicopter will give them a warning to surrender; however, if they decline to surrender, then they will need to accept the consequences of their actions."

The Captain nodded. "There is another squad of tactical response on their way. Please use them how you see fit. They should arrive within an hour or so. Do you need anything from the Sergeant's people or the detectives?"

"No more than what we discussed and what has been agreed. Get rid of the press people and block the roads to stop the traffic. We go in at seven p.m. this evening. The only difference is we will use all our sniper teams."

"Gentlemen, please take all care, and I don't want any of our people being injured or, heaven forbid, worse. If I get any further information, I will phone it through to you immediately. Thank you."

They all filed out the door into the squad room and closed the Captain's door.

They all turned to the constable and asked, "Where does the Captain get his information from?"

The constable replied that she was not at liberty to disclose that but to trust him, as the information he was getting was always correct.

"Constable Wilkens."

"Yes, sir."

"Where did you put the snitch?"

"Put her in the drunk tank, Captain. No matter how we clean the place, it always smells of urine, vomit, and disinfectant."

"Right. Get her phone and find out her name for me."

"Already got all her details, Captain."

A piece of memo pad was handed over.

"Bloody hell. I know her father. Have done since grade three. I will call her father, have a chat with him, and get him to come down to the station. When he arrives, I want you, Constable, and you, Chief Detective, to sit in on the meeting, and if I give you the nod, start to interrogate her. How do these young kids get themselves into such a mess? Thanks, Constable, Chief Detective. I will keep you informed of what is happening. In the meantime, ensure she has food and water, but leave her where she is for the time being."

The two officers left the Captain's office while he searched his phone for her father's number.

The Captain found his old mate's number and pressed dial.

The phone was answered in a moment.

"Hello, Captain. Long time no talk. What can I help you with?"

"More to the point, Andrew, is what I am ringing you about. I don't have good news for you. We have arrested your daughter on criminal charges."

There was stony silence on the phone.

"You must be mistaken, Captain. You must have the wrong person. My daughter works at the courthouse."

"No mistake, Andrew. Now we need to work out what we are going to do with her.

Please come down to the police station to see me. Grab a file and come in through the front door like you have some paperwork to be signed, and the constable will bring you through to my office. Just come by yourself and, at this stage, leave your wife out of the loop. Please don't bring any lawyer, as that will escalate the whole case, and it will be taken out of my hands. Do you understand?"

"Yes, Captain, I will be there in thirty minutes, and thank you for calling me."

The Captain went and made himself a cup of tea and grabbed a couple of shortbread biscuits.

The Captain was just finishing his mug of tea and biscuits when the constable knocked on the door.

"Your friend, the snitch's father, is here, Captain."

"Show a little compassion, Constable, and bring him through. Get the Chief Detective as well."

"Yes, sir."

A few minutes later, the two officers and the girl's father came into the office.

"Sit down, Andrew."

"Let me introduce these two officers. This is Constable Wilkens and Chief Detective Browning. Let everyone sit down, please, and close the door. Andrew, let me bring you up to speed.

At a farm out of town, we have discovered a crack manufacturing facility. This will be shut down in a very short time. In the course of our investigations, we found that the criminal gang had an informer in the courthouse whose job was to let them know if any search warrants were procured for their facility.

We were informed that your daughter was the informer, and today, when we applied for a search warrant, she immediately rang the crack house to let them know that a search warrant had been issued. She was caught in the act of phoning the criminal gang by these two officers. We were able to stop the warning from reaching the gang; otherwise, our assault team would be facing armed resistance when they executed the search warrant.

Now, this is a very serious crime. She would have also signed a declaration that she would not disclose any information on any legal matter that came into her possession while working at the courthouse.

She is eighteen years old, so she is legally an adult. We have no obligation to call you; however, you are an old friend of mine, and I have no wish to see such a young person go to jail, where she will become hardened and end up in a life of crime. She must be punished, and that is outside the jurisdiction of the police force. However, we can make a recommendation to the courts that she be given a community-based sentence if she cooperates with the police and gives us every bit of information she has.

We have incarcerated her in the drunk tank here at the station to give her an understanding of what prison will be like, and we can legally keep her here for seventy-two hours before charging her. A night in the cells will be good for her.

I don't want your wife here bawling her eyes out and insisting that it is all a mistake. It is not a mistake, and your daughter has to recognize that she has committed a criminal act. If you agree, I would like you to go with the Chief Detective and the Constable and sit in on our interrogation.

Are you in agreement, Andrew?"

"Yes, Captain. Her mother has spoiled her for her whole life to the point that she feels entitled to everything. I am sorry this has happened and that you and your people have been inconvenienced by her actions."

"Andrew, it is not up to you to apologize; you have done nothing wrong. It is up to your daughter to apologize and amend her ways. Otherwise, she will end up in jail. Constable, Chief Detective, take

Andrew down to the cell, collect his daughter, and take her to an interview room. Get every bit of information she has about our friends in the crack manufacturing facility. You might also tell her about some of the fatalities we have attended caused by this evil drug."

The girl's father stood up along with the two police officers and, humbled, offered his hand to the Captain.

The Captain stood up and took his hand. "I know this is hard, Andrew, but you have to be tough in this instance. The time for saying that everything will be all right has passed."

Chapter 26
MORE TACTICAL RESPONSE

The captain sat down and looked at the time. Four PM.

"Right, I will head out to the farm and see what is happening."

He checked his bulletproof vest, his Glock handgun, and spare magazines. He opened his office door and asked, "Is the sergeant out at the farm?"

Heads nodded.

"Right, who is the best pistol shot here in this room?"

All eyes swivelled to one of the detectives.

"Have you got a bulletproof vest and handgun on you? It can be a bit dangerous driving around with me."

This brought a few laughs as the pair headed for the car park.

The captain stopped at the front gate as the news crews came running over.

The captain held up his hand, and silence reigned.

"Yes, you."

"Captain, another helicopter has landed, and more tactical response officers have arrived. Can you tell us why?"

"Yes. Things have been taken to a new threat level by my superiors in Sydney, so we have thrown a cordon right around the farm out there. We have found two sets of remains, and we believe that there are more buried there. And I am tired of being shot at. Let me get away so I can go to the farm and have the forensic people bring me up to date. Thank you."

The captain, his detective, and the tactical response officer settled in for the drive to the farm.

Another beautiful autumn day. An Indian summer day, as the Yanks call them.

Thirty minutes later, they arrived, and it was the same thing all over again—news people all wanting more information. The captain waved them off, and the patrol officers cleared the access to the farm.

They all exited the police car, and the captain went across to the tactical response officer.

"Hello, Captain. Everything is ready for us as soon as the sun goes down. We have been watching the farmhouse crack manufacturing facility, and I feel sure they are keeping an eye on us as well. Let's send the forensic people out of here along with the backhoe operator and any other non-essential personnel. I also want these press people to move as well, so we might pass on the info to them that we are finished out here for a few days until the lab in Sydney gives us the nod to restart working."

"Where is the sergeant?"

"Right here, Captain."

"OK, knock off the forensic people and send them back down the road a ways so it looks like we have finished here. You might also go out and give the press people the word that we will hold a press conference in town at 7 PM and that they are all to clear the road as they are a traffic hazard. If we post a few tactical people around the place, it will look like we are just going home a bit early."

"OK, Captain."

The sergeant moved off to start getting people packed and away from the farm. The captain headed out to the gate entrance to the farm and instructed the press people to move their vehicles back into town as they had become a traffic hazard and that the site was being closed for a couple of days while the lab in Sydney caught up with some of the testing. The press people started to pack up and drive back to town reluctantly.

It was coming close to dark by the time they had everyone removed from the site and the road.

Without night vision equipment, it was too dark to see what was happening anywhere about the place. The tactical response people were in contact with their chopper and with their colleagues, and everyone was getting nervous as the clock ticked down to seven PM.

Chapter 27

RAID ON THE CRACK HOUSE

The whole area was deathly quiet, with just the hoot of an owl as they all looked at the clock ticking down to seven PM.

The captain, the detective, and one tactical response officer were in a patrol vehicle parked behind the armoured tactical response vehicle.

The captain counted from ten, and just as it hit five, the armoured vehicle roared out of the farmhouse towards the crack house farm just down the road. The helicopter roared in and hovered at 300 feet above the farm, and all the floodlights from the helicopter lit up the place. A loudspeaker roared out, "Police! Everyone come out of the farmhouse with your hands in the air."

The armoured vehicle stopped seventy-five meters in front of the farmhouse, and the troopers poured out, spreading out as they approached the farmhouse. The two criminals acting as lookouts swung their Uzi submachine pistols up and started to fire at the helicopter. There were four louder cracks from the sniper rifles, and both guards went down.

The captain's phone buzzed. It was the Time Walker. Before the captain could say anything, the Time Walker spoke urgently.

"The machine gun has been mounted in the trees to the left of the road, Captain."

The captain spoke into his radio. "Machine gun in the trees to the left of the armoured vehicle."

All the tactical response officers went flat on the ground and turned toward the possible location just as the booming thunder of a fully automatic 7.62mm machine gun opened up, with the first burst tearing the air above the troopers' heads.

The gunner never got another chance to correct his aim as eight Heckler & Koch 5.25 automatic weapons poured a hail of fire at the location where the machine gun was positioned.

A voice came over the radio. "The two officers closest, check out that weapon and make sure it does not get used again. The rest of you, into the farmhouse. Flash bangs and tear gas. Anyone with a weapon in their hands, put them down."

The captain, his detective, and the trooper were taking cover behind the police vehicle when the captain realized that the Time Walker was still on the phone.

He was about to hang up when he thought he would just check if the young bloke had hung up.

"Hello?"

"Captain, the guy with the RPG is creeping around behind the trees towards the main road so he can get a shot at the rear of the armoured vehicle."

"OK. We will sort him out. Guys, come with me. There is another guy with an RPG coming around behind us. No shooting unless I give the word."

The only one with night vision was the trooper, so they all followed him back towards the main road.

The trooper held up his hand. The captain and the detective stopped. The trooper knelt down on one knee, followed by the two police officers. They could hear the cacophony of gunfire coming from the house while they waited. The next moment, the criminal with the RPG walked right up to them without seeing them.

Three barrels were poked into him, and he stopped in his tracks.

"Drop the weapon. Police here."

Both his hands shot into the air, and the RPG dropped to the ground. He was not going to argue with three barrels poking into him.

"Handcuff him and drag him out to the access road. And bring that RPG. I want to know where they got a heavy machine gun and an RPG from."

The captain and the trooper headed towards the farmhouse, keeping the armoured vehicle between them and the front of the farmhouse. The gunfire had stopped, and people were spilling out the front door with their hands in the air. Their eyes were streaming from the tear gas. They could hear the all-clear one by one as they searched the house.

Four troopers were searching the farm shed, and the clatter of the chopper overhead made for a deafening scenario. The second chopper was circling around the farmhouse about 200 meters away, just in case anybody made a run for the bush.

The leader of the tactical response team came up to the captain.

"All my men are accounted for without any injuries. The two guards who fired at the chopper are both dead, as are the two men who were manning the machine gun. One idiot inside the house decided to have a go at my men. He was killed as well. The rest of the people are mainly chemists, with a couple of military types. We will get the paddy wagon up here and get them locked away and back to town to the cells. We are doing body searches now to ensure that they don't have any hidden weapons. Captain, your call on the machine gun saved us from getting any injuries. How did you know it had been taken out of the farmhouse and set up on our flank?"

"My own personal informant keeps me well informed on what is happening. I hope one day to meet up with him, as I have never met him, but he has my phone number, and he watches over me—for which I am thankful. Now, we have a lot of work for the forensic people again. Do we need an ambulance at all for the prisoners?"

They all walked down to the group standing with their hands in the air.

The captain called up the sergeant on the radio and informed him it was all over and they needed to get the prisoners back to town.

"The fire truck can go back as well."

The trooper captain asked if anybody needed medical assistance.

"Better bring the ambulance down here because they all have tear gas in their eyes. Better that than being dead, though."

The sergeant escorted the two ambulances to the farmhouse, and the first responders started treating tear gas eyes before the prisoners were escorted to the paddy wagon.

Slowly, the tension drained away from the site. The coroner arrived to pick up the dead bodies of the criminals. Cameras were flashing everywhere. Generators were set up and running, and floodlights lit up the whole scene.

Forensic teams were measuring the whole scene and collecting spent cartridges.

The captain walked over to where the machine gun was set up. "Tell me, where did these guys get an M60 firing 7.62mm rounds? These weapons, like the RPG, are not available to the public. We need to do some investigations into this weapon supply."

Looking down at the two bodies, the captain saw multiple wounds from the hail of fire from the tactical response troopers.

"I am glad that was not me on the receiving end of that fusillade," he muttered.

He got out of the way of the forensic people and the coroner so they could do their work.

The captain found a seat out of the way and took out his phone, dialling the Commissioner in Sydney.

The phone only rang once before the Commissioner was on the line.

"Yes, Captain. How did the raid go?"

"All our people are safe and well, sir."

"Thank God for that. What about the bad guys?"

"Five dead, sir. Two who opened fire on the helicopters with Uzi submachine guns, two operating an M60 machine gun that opened fire on the troops, plus one idiot inside the house trying to be a hero, taking on a half-dozen tactical response people with an Uzi. The young fellow gave me a warning that the machine gun had been moved from the house out into the tree line, so we were able to avoid any casualties among our people. It is tragic that five people had to be shot and killed; however, they did not give us any choice and ignored the police warning by loudspeaker from the helicopter and calls from the officers."

"Very well, Captain. The raids here in Sydney are still underway, but I believe we will have a good result from this operation. Good night, Captain."

The captain was left holding a dead phone and was about to slip it back into his pocket when it rang again.

It was his mate, the Time Walker.

"Hello, young fellow. Thank you for the tip-off on the machine gun—it saved police lives. However, the bad guys suffered five dead. Now, this is not your fault, as these people persist in ignoring warnings and firing at officers doing their duty."

"Captain, they are truly evil people who prey on the defenceless members of society. Are you OK?"

"Yes, thank you."

"Good night, Captain. Talk tomorrow. Stay safe."

He was gone again.

The captain shook his head. He would dearly like to meet this young fellow, as he owed him so much, but it looked like that was not going to happen.

"Sergeant."

"Yes, sir?"

"I seem to make a lot of work for you and the forensic people, so I will leave it in your capable hands and go back to face the horde at the police station. By now, they'll be well aware that something has happened out here."

"Better you than me, sir."

"Bring that machine gun and RPG into the station after forensics have finished with them, thank you."

"Aye, aye, Captain."

The captain, his detective driver, and the bodyguard climbed into their vehicle and headed back to the police station.

Thirty minutes later, they arrived at the station—only to find the street blocked with TV vans and people milling about everywhere.

"Just take a look at this rabble, will you?" the captain muttered.

"Flick on the flashing lights and push your way through. Give me that microphone."

He took the microphone and spoke with authority.

"This is Captain Wilson. Please clear the street so traffic can get through and emergency vehicles have access. Any vehicle still on the road in five minutes will be impounded and taken to our lock-up yard. I will give a brief press conference in ten minutes."

The road cleared slowly, allowing the police car to access the station's rear yard.

The captain walked through the back door with the detective and his trooper bodyguard. To his surprise, the constable and the detectives were still there.

The constable was the first to speak.

"Please, Captain, how is everybody? How did the operation go?"

"Everyone is safe and well, though we cannot say the same for the bad guys—five dead after firing at the chopper and opening up with a heavy machine gun on the tactical boys. A well-planned and executed operation, but still tragic that there was a loss of life."

He paused, glancing at the constable.

"I'd like you, Constable, and your chief detective to join me now in facing the horde of press outside—so I'm not left alone to face their wrath for sending them back to town away from the operation tonight."

Chapter 28
PRESS CONFERENCE

With that, the Captain, the two officers, and his tactical response bodyguard headed out to the front of the station. The moment the door of the station opened; it was like the baying of wolves around a sheep carcass.

The captain held up his hands for silence, but the noise did not abate, so he turned to go back into the station. Silence reigned instantly.

"Right, I will only speak to the press if the press acts civilized. Now, let me try and bring you all up to date on events today.

We moved everyone away from the farm this afternoon as we had planned a raid on the farmhouse across the road, as we discovered that the place was being used for the manufacture of drugs. We did not want anybody exposed to stray bullets in the event of the criminals not surrendering. We raided the place at 7 p.m. this evening with three squads of tactical response personnel and two helicopters. The farmhouse was heavily defended by paramilitary-type personnel armed with automatic weapons and anti-tank weapons. It was only the skill of the police unit that allowed the raid to succeed without any police casualties.

However, the persons at the farmhouse resisted with heavy machine-gun fire and refused to surrender, and those people were unfortunately killed during the firefight.

The farm across the road, where we have been exhuming the remains of victims, is an ongoing operation as we have a lot of work ahead of us yet, until we can say with certainty that there are no more persons buried there.

The forensic people have a big task ahead of them to identify these remains as we don't know where they came from. The remains are being treated with all the respect due to young lives lost and now found to be returned to their loved ones.

Now, any questions?"

Hands went up everywhere.

"Right, you, Miss, what is your question?"

"Why were you the subject of a drive-by attempt the other night, and who are the shooters?"

"Right, we are not sure why I have been singled out, but we believe that it was planned by the drug people. We have identified the shooters, but we will not disclose their names in respect of their families, who had nothing to do with the shooting. The pair were not long released from gaol for crimes of violence.

Next question?"

"How many victims have you found out at the farm?"

"We have exhumed two victims at this time, with what we believe are more gravesites to be investigated."

"Next question."

"Captain, do you feel remorse about the people who have been killed by the police in the last couple of days?"

"Listen, all of you. I and my men do not go about shooting people just because we have a handgun and the authority to wear it. The people who attacked me outside my house did so to kill me. It was them or my next-door neighbour and myself. Tonight, five criminals were killed in a shootout because they elected to shoot at the helicopters and the tactical response personnel. They were not shooting blanks like in a video game. They had automatic weapons, and two of them had an M60 heavy machine gun, which they started to fire at the response group. My men did what was necessary to neutralize the danger to themselves and their comrades. Does everyone understand that?"

Silence reigned.

"Good night, everyone," as the Captain turned and walked away, accompanied by his officers back into the station.

"Bloody twits, some of them," mumbled the Captain.

"Constable, I know it has been a long day, but could you grab the Chief Detective and come to my office, please?"

"Yes, sir."

Five minutes later, the Captain had a cup of tea and was joined by his two colleagues.

"There is more work for the Chief Detective from this drug bust. I want to know how and where these druggies got their automatic weapons. You are going to find pushback from the army because there is only one place that has M60 machine guns, and they are not going to like you prying into their dirty linen."

"Not a problem, Captain, as I have some good contacts with the Federal Police, and they will want to know where as well."

"All right. I know you are all getting a lot of work to do the last few days, but we have done some great work as a team and put a lot of bad people on the defensive. Now, how is our young snitch, Constable?"

"Captain, she spent time with us and her father, and we got every piece of information possible out of her. I do apologize, Captain. She is just a young kid who has been told all her life she is something special and then has gone to work and found out she is not so special after all."

"Is anything that she has told you useful in our investigation, Chief Detective?"

"Not really, sir. She was just a small cog in a big drug ring, and she really had no idea what she was doing. The $100 a week was all she saw when it was offered."

"Right, let's leave her where she is until tomorrow morning, then call her father and release her. I will speak to the Chief Magistrate before we let her go and the Chief Prosecutor and see just what we charge her with. Her father can then get a solicitor if he wishes, and we can release her on bail. She is the least of my concerns at the moment. Thank you for everything you have done over the last few days."

It was time to call it a day.

The day shift headed out the doors.

They both stood up just as the Captain's hand phone rang again.

Chapter 29

SERIAL RAPIST VICTIM

"Captain Wilson here."

"Captain, call the chief detective and the constable back into the office, please."

"Constable, chief detective, another moment please."

"Firstly, Captain, the reward has allowed me to upgrade my equipment, and it is sooo much better now. Right, the constable needs to go to 631 Kingston Street and speak to a young lady there who was raped the other evening. She did not tell her mother; however, she still has her underwear, and she should go and see a doctor immediately. Now, the detective should find a reason to arrest the reporter with the man bun and blond beard from the local rag. He spiked her drink at the disco, then took her home via the back road, where he raped her and beat her savagely, where her mother cannot see the injuries. She was too embarrassed to tell her mother what had happened. Now, Captain, boot up your computer and have the constable and the detective watch what I am going to show you. I can now email my videos without using memory sticks. This has been edited to take out the worst parts. Once again, for your eyes only."

The Captain booted up his desktop and indicated to the two officers to come around the desk and watch the video coming through.

Five minutes later, the three of them were silent as what they had seen was horrific.

"You still there, young fella?"

"Yes, Captain. I have saved the video to your hard drive under today's date. This is the upgrade of my equipment that I was able to do with the reward money. Please take this animal off the streets. Look at the bottom of the email that I sent you, and you will find a photo of the rapist. Don't forget to get a DNA test from the guy, and you will solve some other cold rape cases around the district."

"We will work out a plan as soon as you hang up."

"Sorry, Captain. Did not realize that I was holding you up."

The phone went dead.

The Captain looked at the two officers, who were ashen-faced.

"I want this animal locked up till he is an old man. Constable, you will need to talk to the young lady and get her to understand that we need to take this animal off the streets, and we need her help to do it. Sounds like he has been at this sort of thing for a while."

"It's getting late, but we really should get this girl into the hospital."

"We are on it, Captain."

"Right. 631 Kingston Street is where she lives with her mother and father. I don't know her name, but I am sure that you will work it out. If you need me for anything, just call me at any time. I have sent the photo through to the printer. Pick it up and take it with you."

"We are on our way, Captain."

The captain could not believe how busy they were. The Time Walker seemed to be doing nothing but finding crimes for them to clean up: unsolved missing persons, crack houses, and now a serial rapist.

Chapter 30

MEETING THE RAPE VICTIM

The two police officers got a car and headed across town. Twenty minutes later, they stopped in front of 631 Kingston Street.

They exited the police vehicle, and both of them stood there, looking at the suburban house.

"Well, they have their name on the letterbox, so that makes it easier.

Come on, chief detective, let me do the talking. We don't want you scaring the young lady any more than what she is now."

The pair walked up and rang the doorbell and waited.

They could hear the chime of the doorbell inside the house. Nice gardens and a well-kept house.

The front door opened, and a woman about forty-five years of age stood there.

"Oh, my goodness, the police. What can I help you with?"

"Mrs. Jackson, is your daughter at home?"

"Yes, constable, however, she is not feeling well. She has been sick since last Saturday morning."

"I understand that, Mrs. Jackson. However, it is very important that I speak with her for a few minutes."

"She is in bed, constable, and I can't get her to go see the doctor. I am not sure what is wrong with her."

"Mrs. Jackson, your daughter must speak with myself or another police officer, and better that she speaks to me. I will only take a few minutes, but it is a very important police matter."

"Well, all right, I will take you through. Please come this way."

"Constable, I will stay here until you need me." The chief detective knew that the constable was better for this sort of business.

The girl's mother was puzzled about the behaviour of the two police personnel.

"This is her room here. I will let Angie know you are here."

The constable placed her hand on the mother's arm. "Please let me speak to her alone. I promise to call you if there is any problem."

The mother nodded but was unsure what was happening.

The constable opened the door and stepped into the room and closed the door quietly.

The girl was half asleep, almost comatose. "Angie, my name is Constable Wilkins, and we know what that animal did to you last Saturday on the way home. We are here to help you and to make sure that he does not hurt any other girl like he has done to you.

I know your mother does not know what happened, but it is not your fault. You are not to blame for your injuries."

The girl looked at the constable and burst into tears. The constable took her hand and sat down on the chair beside the bed.

"Angie, is it all right for me to call you that?"

The girl nodded her head, still sobbing. The constable took her in her arms and hugged her.

"Tell me if you are in any pain from me holding you."

"I am in pain all over, constable. He beat me and punched me, but I can't tell Mum, as Dad would say it is all my fault."

"You leave that up to me to tell your parents. These people who drug young girls work on the principle that their victims won't tell their parents, so they keep doing it again and again to unsuspecting girls just out having a good time. Now, can you have a look at this photo? Is this the man?"

Showing the girl the photo of the rapist brought on another bout of sobbing as she nodded her head in agreement.

"We will have him arrested tomorrow morning, and he is going away for a long time. We believe that this is not the first time he has done this sort of thing. Now, you have to go to the hospital and have these injuries examined. You could have internal bleeding; will you let me call an ambulance for you?"

"Yes, please, officer. I feel like I am going to die."

"Well, that is not going to happen, as I will be helping you all the way. OK?"

The constable stood up. "I will just talk to my colleague and get him to call an ambulance, and I will ride with you to the hospital. OK?"

A nod of the head.

"Now, do you still have your underwear from last Saturday evening?"

The constable had her fingers crossed.

"Yes, Miss. I bagged all my clothes and hid them away from Mum and Dad at the bottom of the wardrobe."

The constable called the chief detective in for a moment to witness the search of the wardrobe. There was a black rubbish bag there with the top tied.

"Is this it, Angie?"

A nod of Angie's head to say yes.

The officers went outside and quietly closed the door.

"Mrs. Jackson, could you please come out here to the lounge? I need to talk to you."

"Officers, what is happening?" asked a very confused mother.

"Please sit down. Chief detective, please call for an ambulance and have our social worker standing by. Now, Mrs. Jackson, last Saturday evening while your daughter was out enjoying herself with a few friends, an animal spiked her drink with what is known as a rape drug. He offered her a lift home as she was feeling sick; however, along the way, he savagely beat and raped her, but he is cunning and did not leave a visible mark on her where it could be seen.

Your daughter is going to be taken to the hospital as we believe she could have internal injuries. She has also identified the person who did this to her, and we will arrest him and charge him with the crime tomorrow morning. She is terrified that her father will blame her for what happened. She needs a lot of love and sympathy, not a parent who is going to blame her for being the victim of a crime. Do you understand?"

"Ambulance on its way, and our social worker is coming with the ambulance."

"Thanks, chief."

"You have not answered my question, Mrs. Jackson. Are you going to be there to love and assist your daughter now she needs you badly?"

"Of course, officer. She is my daughter."

"Where is your husband at this time, Mrs. Jackson?"

"He will not be home for another few hours, as he works late in the business every night doing the bookwork."

"What about your husband? Will he be there as well for your daughter?"

"You just leave her father to me. If he starts any of his nonsense, he will be looking for a divorce lawyer and be out living on the street. Now, may I see my daughter, please?"

The constable stood up and led her back to the daughter's bedroom.

The daughter burst into tears again. "I'm sorry, Mum."

"It is not your fault, love. You did nothing wrong, and the police will arrest the animal who has hurt you. Now let your Mum give you a hug."

The constable looked out the window to see an ambulance pull up outside the house.

"Well, she will help us get this animal. Let the ambulance people in, Chief."

They opened the door to admit an ambulance officer and the social worker.

"Hello, Constable. Still getting the dirty work, I see."

"Yes, now come this way and meet Angie. She is tougher than most people think. We know who did this, but we need Angie's help as well. You know the story better than me."

The professionals swung into action and slid Angie onto a stretcher. The social worker was introduced and gave Angie a hug, saying she would be with her the whole time until she was passed out, fit and well.

Within thirty minutes, the street was back to normal, and the curious neighbours had all gone back into their houses.

The two police officers went back to the police station and forced their way back through the newspeople.

The pair went into the Captain's office and knocked on the door.

"Working late again. Hopefully, people, we will catch up soon. How was the young lady?"

"Like we thought, Captain. Frightened of her father blaming her."

"Tomorrow, arrest the animal at the newspaper for assault until we get the result back on the DNA sample we take and send to Sydney to compare to cold cases around the country. We might get enough results from previous rape cases to not need the young lady's evidence at this time.

Now, let's all go home and get some sleep."

Chapter 31

THE SNITCH'S PARENTS

It was seven a.m. the next morning when the Captain arrived at the police station.

"Good morning, everyone. Many thanks for a successful raid last evening. I want to thank everyone for the hard work that has gone into the events that have happened over the last few days. Forensics— have we been able to identify any of the dead from the raid last night?"

"Yes, Captain. All of them have previous criminal records for drugs and violence, so it was only a matter of time before they were caught up in something like last evening."

"Right, I want to get the young lady from the cells as soon as I can get her parents here in the station. We need to ensure that all the chemists have been fingerprinted and check with immigration if they are legal in the country. Check with the courthouse when we can get them before the courts. I suppose all the do-gooders will be here soon saying the poor buggers could not get any other work.

We need to try and find out where the heavy weapons came from. If the army has a bad egg selling machine guns, it's also probable that he has sold some to other crime cartels.

Have we been able to tie the two shooters who were using me for target practice back to the drug house?"

"Captain, we are waiting for forensics to finish checking for fingerprints through the drug house. If their fingerprints turn up there, then we can say with certainty that it was the drug people trying to get rid of you."

"Chief detective, go and arrest that sleazebag at the local newspaper as soon as it opens.

OK. Any questions? Right, call me if anything comes up."

The Captain made a cup of tea and went inside to phone the snitch's father.

"Good morning, Captain."

"Hello, Andrew. Could you and your wife come down to the station and have a word with me, please?"

"We are on our way, Captain."

The Captain sat down and drank his tea in silence.

It was not long before the snitch's father and mother were shown into the Captain's office.

"Constable, please stay if you would. Please sit down, Andrew, Mavis. Would either of you like a tea or coffee?"

Two heads shook no.

"All right, as I explained yesterday, Andrew, your daughter needed to be taught a lesson that crime does not pay. We raided the drug house where she was involved last night. Five persons are dead from the shootout, and we are lucky that none of them were police officers. I have spoken to our crown prosecutor, and he does not want to make a case out of her actions as she is such a low person in the whole operation.

That does not mean that she can get off scot-free, as she also broke a signed confidential agreement with her employer, the court system, which carries a substantial fine and possible jail time. I don't want to push this matter any further as we have a lot more serious matters on our hands at the moment, and she has spent the night in the cells, so she knows a little of what prison could be like. No more mollycoddling her. She is an adult and must be responsible for her actions. Is that understood, Andrew?"

A nod of the head.

"Mavis?" Another nod of the head.

"I am going to release her. However, I doubt that the magistrate will allow her to come back to her position at the courthouse. It might be best if she just quietly resigned and looked for another position. Constable, could you bring the young lady here from the cells along with her possessions, please?"

The constable disappeared and returned within 10 minutes with their young daughter.

She was ushered into the Captain's office.

"Good morning, young lady. Not very nice in the cells, is it?"

"No, sir."

"We are releasing you into the custody of your parents, even though you are an adult. You are fortunate that you have people who care about you. Five persons died last night from the drug ring that you were telephoning yesterday. If you persist in breaking the law, you will end up in jail. Is that understood? There is no easy money in this world, just dirty money. Don't get involved again, or you might not be so lucky next time. Is that understood?"

"Yes, sir."

"Right, go home with your parents, have a shower, change your clothes, and have some decent food, then sit down with your parents and give thanks for your release. Good day. I don't wish to see you again in my police station."

"Thank you, Andrew, for being here for her. Good day."

The family filed out under the guidance and curious eyes of the constable and the squad room of detectives.

The captain's phone rang.

The Captain did not even need to look to see it was The Time Walker.

"Good morning, young fellow. Did I do wrong letting her go without trying to have her locked up?"

"No, Captain. You do not disappoint me at all. Why destroy a young person for a minor charge? She will not step out of line again. I will keep an eye on her from time to time to make sure that she treads the straight and narrow."

"Well, young fellow, the detectives have gone to pick up the rapist. I hope he has not done a runner."

"I am keeping an eye on him, and he will wander down to the local newspaper soon after picking up a coffee. I am watching the newspaper office and will send you a copy of his arrest. It will be all denials; however, his DNA will convict him and send him away for a long time."

"Is there anything else, young fellow?"

"Not today, Captain. Please try and catch up with the exhuming of the bodies out at the farm. I am investigating a few other crimes that you will need to investigate soon. Have a nice day, Captain."

Chapter 32

ARRESTING THE SERIAL RAPIST

Two detectives drove downtown to the local newspaper office in an unmarked police vehicle and parked across the street.

They walked across and checked the front door; however, it was still locked, and the hours-of-business sign said there were another 30 minutes before opening.

"Well, let's get a coffee and a muffin from the coffee shop down the road, and we'll keep an eye on the place until it opens and the suspect arrives."

"You won me. Is this bloke expected to be violent, or do you think he'll come along peacefully?"

"Mate, as far as I'm concerned, they all have the potential to get violent if they're looking at being done for a crime that'll put them away for a few years. From what I understand from the Captain, this guy has been making a habit of beating girls and raping them, so we'll have our Tasers ready if he starts to act up at all."

By this time, they were at the coffee shop, which had an outdoor counter with tables and chairs where they could sit and still see the front and side entrances to the newspaper office.

Two coffees and two muffins later, they were seated and watching the office. The pair discussed the events of the previous week or so.

The unmarked graves, the crack house raid, the shootings at the Captain—it was all a lot to take in, and now this serial rapist as well.

The weather was perfect: sunny and bright. The two detectives were just finishing their coffee when they saw a woman opening the door to the newspaper office.

"Looks like we're in business, mate. Let's find out what time our friend will arrive. I don't see anyone along the street that looks like him, so we might get some information from the woman who just opened the place up."

The duo crossed the road and caught the door before it could shut and latch.

The woman was surprised.

"We're not open yet. The office doesn't open for another 30 minutes."

Both detectives showed their badges.

"Oh, police."

"Good morning. I'm Chief Detective Browning, and this is Detective Johnson."

Holding up the print of the alleged rapist, they asked, "Do you know this man?"

"Yes," was the reply. "That's the boss's son. What's he done now?"

"Why should it be 'what's he done now?'"

"Well, his father is always bailing him out of trouble of one sort or another. His father is a real gentleman, not like his son, who's a real sleazebag."

Both detectives looked at each other.

"What's his name, if you don't mind my asking?"

"His name is Con Atkins, and this is my last week here, and he can find some other poor woman to put up with the touching and rubbing up against from him."

"Tell me, is that side door locked?"

"Yes, detective. We never open it except for deliveries."

"Good. We'll leave you now and keep an eye on the place for when our friend Con arrives. We have some questions we want answers to."

The two detectives went back to their vehicle and sat, waiting for their suspect to wander in, as the woman had said he does.

Half an hour went by when they saw him coming down the street with a takeaway coffee in hand and ear buds in his ears, strolling along without a care in the world.

"Looks like he has no worries at all, doesn't he?" said the lead detective.

"Well, me bucko, that's all about to change for you."

Con, the newsman, wandered up and opened the door to the newspaper office.

The two detectives were across the road and once again caught the door before it latched shut.

"Mr. Atkins. A moment, please. We'd like a word with you."

Neither detective was ready for the reaction of the alleged rapist, who hurdled the front counter and grabbed the woman in the office with one arm around her neck. A knife appeared in his other hand and was pressed against her throat. This all happened so quickly that neither detective had a chance to grab him or to draw a Taser and shoot him with it.

"Get back, or she gets her throat cut."

"Calm down, Mr. Atkins. We just want a word with you. No need to get violent with the lady."

"I know what you coppers are like. A word turns into a bashing, and then I get blamed for something I didn't do."

"Well, using a knife puts you into the assault with a deadly weapon class, and if you harm the lady, it'll get a lot worse, so put the knife down, and let's all have a chat."

"Shut up, copper. Give me the key to the side door, Maureen. You coppers stay right where you are, or she gets another set of lips to breathe out of."

Maureen reached into the pocket of her dress and pulled out a ring of keys, handing them to Con.

"You unlock the door, Maureen. I'm not taking my eyes off these two cops."

Maureen fumbled with the keys.

"C'mon, Maureen, open the door. Stop mucking about."

Maureen finally got the door unlocked.

"It's unlocked, Con. You can let me go now."

"Right, throw the keys over there to the cop so he can lock the front door."

Maureen tossed the keys to the detective next to the door.

"Right, lock the door from the inside so you guys can't follow me."

The detective locked the door as directed.

"Throw the keys back to Maureen and no funny stuff, or she gets slashed."

Maureen caught the keys.

"Now, Maureen, I'm going to go out through the side door and pull it shut, then I'll lock it from the outside so none of you can get out. You cops sit on the floor, facing the front door. That'll slow you down getting up to grab me."

Both detectives turned and sat on the floor as instructed.

Con opened the door and, still watching the police inside, pushed Maureen across the room.

The next moment, he felt the worst pain he had ever felt. His whole body jerked and juddered before he collapsed to the floor and flopped about like a fish out of water.

Both detectives were up and coming around the counter when they saw the constable.

"Thank you, constable. While he's still out of it, put your handcuffs on the little weasel. If he starts to give you any trouble, give him another belt from your Taser."

"Maureen, are you all right?"

"Yes, officer."

"Maureen, we'd like you to come down to the station and give us a statement about what has happened. That way, we can keep him in remand, and the magistrate won't allow him out on bail as he is a threat to you and other witnesses."

"No problem, officer. The little slimebag would have slashed me if it suited him. I'll close the office and be down at the police station in about 20 minutes."

The officers left Maureen to lock up while they dragged the inert form of Con, the rapist-turned-would-be-slasher, out to the paddy wagon and threw him in the back. A small crowd had gathered to see what was going on.

"All right, folks, nothing else to see, so can you all go about your business?"

The crowd slowly broke up and left the scene, all talking and trying to work out what was going on.

"Tell me, constable, why were you just conveniently standing outside the door with your Taser in your hand, waiting to zap the slimebag?"

"Well, detective, a little bird told me that you guys needed a helping hand from the uniform branch, so I was the closest. I got to come to your rescue."

"Well, constable, we are grateful. However, I don't think we'll hear the end of this episode for a while."

They were all soon back at the station, and the Captain came down to the cells to have a look at the prisoner.

"Right, fingerprint him and get a DNA sample. Get the samples away to Sydney as soon as possible. I don't want this guy getting out on bail. If he gives you any trouble and refuses to give a sample, Taser him again. If his father turns up here at the station, please bring him to me in my office. I believe his father has been getting him out of all sorts of scrapes over the last few years."

Con was sitting on the cell bed, still half dazed from the Taser shock.

The forensic person was there in minutes and they fingerprinted and took a DNA swab before Con even knew what was happening.

Back in the office, the Captain mentioned that the Girl in Blue had gotten the detective branch out of trouble.

"Yes, Captain. He was slick as a rat with a gold tooth and jumped the counter and had the knife at the woman's throat before we could grab him."

"Well, that is one more thing to keep him in the cells till he comes to trial. Write it up and book him for assault with a weapon. I'm sure that hostage will be happy to sign a statement to that effect. I'll be in my office if anyone wants me."

Chapter 33

MAUREEN GIVES A STATEMENT

The captain sat down just as his phone rang.

It was forensic at the crack house.

"Captain, we have found a .308 long rifle under a bed, and we have lifted fingerprints from it which match one of the deceased crack house guards. We will need to do a check on the ballistics of the bullet from the police van and this rifle. However, I will just about guarantee that we've got the shooter. We have also found two sets of prints that match the two shooters who tried to take you out the other night. This ties the shooting to the crack house."

"Thank you very much. Good work. That is another loose end tied off. Now I need to get back onto the farm investigation and see if we have any more buried people out there."

The Captain decided to firstly call the police commissioner in Sydney.

The phone only rang a couple of times before being answered.

"Good morning, Captain. What's happening in your part of Australia?"

"Good morning, Commissioner. Well, we believe that we have taken a serial rapist into custody this morning. When my detectives went to speak to him, he took a woman hostage and threatened her with a knife. One of my constables was able to Taser him when he didn't have the knife at the hostage's throat. We will have a DNA sample down to the Sydney laboratory this afternoon, and with a bit of luck, it will tie him into quite a few cold case rapes and assaults on young women around the area. We have enough on him now to get the magistrate to refuse bail after his knife attack until we get the DNA results back from the lab. I will contact Justice Williams and bring him up to date on the crack house raid and the arrest of our rapist as soon as we finish this conversation. We also believe that one of the deceased at the crack house is the shooter who took a couple of shots at myself and the constable. We have, we believe, the .308 long rifle with the fingerprints of one of the deceased guards. We have also found the fingerprints in the crack house of the two shooters who tried to take me out the other evening. I will be sending the two bodyguards back to Sydney as they are no longer required."

"Well, Captain, your area has been very busy of late. Send two of the tactical response teams and one helicopter back to Sydney as soon as you are happy that you no longer need them. Keep one team, and I want to keep a bodyguard on yourself and your wife for another week at least. Keep looking out on the farm for further remains so we can say that we have found all the remains that are buried there. When we have identified them all, this will bring closure to so many families. Then we need to find the culprits who took them from their families. You still have a lot of work ahead of you, Captain. Good day."

There was a knock on the door.

"Come in."

"Captain, Maureen from the newspaper office has just arrived and is writing out a statement regarding the incident. Would you like to speak to her for a moment?"

"Please bring her here, thank you."

Maureen nervously looked into the captain's office.

"Come in, Maureen. Can I call you Maureen?"

"Yes, Captain."

"It is very good of you to come down here and give us your time to write out a statement for the court so our friend Con is not sprung on bail immediately to threaten yourself or other women."

"Captain, he is not a nice person, whereas his father is a real gentleman."

"Maureen, we will be doing everything in our power to ensure that he does not get released on bail."

"Thank you, Captain. Now I will finish my statement and go back and open the newspaper office."

"Good morning, Maureen, and thank you once again."

"Constable, see if Maureen would like a cup of tea or coffee, thank you."

"No worries, Captain."

The Captain looked up the number of the magistrate, Justice Williams, and called the number.

"Hello, Bill. You making work for me again?"

"Yeah, sorry mate, but we have arrested the son of the owner of the local newspaper for assault with a deadly weapon. We actually went to the newspaper office to have a talk to him about another assault and rape last week, but he jumped the gun on us and took the woman in the office hostage with a knife to her throat. My constable was waiting outside and managed to Taser him when he let his hostage go for a minute. We believe that his DNA will tie into a few cold cases we have on the books, plus we want to get a search warrant to see if he has any trophies in his unit."

"Come on up to the courthouse with the details, and I will get a search warrant sworn out for you. I will be free in about a half hour."

"Thanks, mate."

It was a beautiful autumn day with the sun shining, so the Captain decided to walk the few streets to the courthouse. He closed his laptop and decided to take it with him to his meeting with the magistrate.

His phone rang again.

"Good morning, young fellow."

"Good morning, Captain. I see you are about to go up to the courthouse and get a search warrant for that sleazebag's unit."

"That is correct. Have I done something wrong?"

"No, Captain, it is time to bring the chief magistrate into the picture because you are going to get lawyers soon wanting to bail people like the sleazebag out of jail. Once he has seen the video, he will think twice about giving them bail. He will need to be convinced, though, that what he is seeing is real. I will be watching the courthouse for the next few hours."

The captain had not thought that they would need to convince the magistrate that what he was seeing was real.

"OK, young fellow, I will take my laptop with me, and I am sure that once he sees the video on the rape and assault of the young lady last week, he will be convinced."

"Captain, don't show him the video; otherwise, he will have to recuse himself from the bail application. Just boot up your computer and hand it over to him. I will convince him that what he and you are seeing is the genuine article."

"Very well, young fellow. I had not thought about the problem that would have caused. I am leaving now for the courthouse."

The Captain bagged his laptop and headed out the front door of the police station to be met by the horde of newspaper and television people all wanting information.

The Captain stopped and held up his hands. Silence reigned.

"Good morning, people. The only news that I have for you is that we have found, we believe, the .308 long rifle that was used in the shooting of the police van being driven by Constable Wilkins. The forensic people are checking the fingerprints and ballistics of the weapon as we speak. The fingerprints of the two people killed in the shootout with myself have also been found in the crack farmhouse. As you know, we have found three sets of human remains, and we believe that there are more waiting to be found out on 'Hilltop' farm. I will keep you informed as more information becomes available. Questions?"

"Captain, it was reported that a young man was arrested at the local newspaper office this morning. Is this in relation to the bodies at the farm?"

"No. The gentleman in question was asked to come into the station to assist us with a line of investigation on another matter when he pulled a knife and took the office lady hostage. Once again, it was Constable Wilkins who happened to be in the right place and was able to immobilize the person with a Taser. He has been charged with assault with a deadly weapon and will be remanded in jail while we have DNA tests done. I am on my way now to the courthouse to get a search warrant for his unit. Thank you, and now please stand aside while I walk up to the courthouse on this lovely day."

The captain, along with his tactical response bodyguard, walked through the waiting crowd, who parted like the Red Sea for Moses.

The Captain spoke to his bodyguard.

"What a lovely day. I love Autumn."

Fifteen minutes later, they both arrived at the courthouse. The automatic door swung open as they approached, and there waiting for them was the chief Justice. The bodyguard stepped aside and stood near the door. The Captain shook hands with Andrew and was invited into his chambers for a coffee.

"Good morning, Captain. You've had a busy week, have you not?"

"Without a doubt, Andrew, now where is that coffee that you promised?"

"Coming, mate. Now, what was the story on the arrest at the local newspaper office?"

"Well, Andrew, the owner's son was identified in an assault and rape incident, and two detectives went there to bring him in for questioning. However, he lost the plot, grabbed the office woman, and held a knife to her throat. The two detectives were powerless to do anything. However, he backed out the side door, pushed the office lady back into the office, and made to lock the door. Constable Wilkins was waiting for him outside and jabbed a Taser into his neck and dropped him like a stunned mullet to the floor. He is now residing in the cells, and we have taken a DNA sample, fingerprints, and drug tests, and we are waiting on the results. I believe that he has been using a date-rape drug; however, he also likes to beat his victims very severely, but he beats them where the injuries cannot be seen unless the victim is naked."

Both the men were soon sipping strong coffee made all the better because it was a couple of old friends chatting together.

"Right, Captain, you are going to have a defence lawyer saying that he is the wrong person and should get bail."

"Andrew, is there another magistrate here at the courthouse?"

"Mate, we have five magistrates here now. Town has grown into a small city over the last five years. Why do you want to speak to another magistrate?"

"Well, I want to show you a video about this alleged rapist, but I don't want to risk keeping him in jail until he comes up for trial."

"Well, the assault with a deadly weapon is pretty serious stuff, so it would want to be a good argument for me to release him on bail."

"Andrew, if I had a video of our rapist in action, could I show it to a magistrate to ensure that he was held in remand till his trial, by which time we will have the results of his DNA back? I believe that those results will tie him into other cold rape cases."

"Mate, the assault with a knife will be enough to keep him on remand till he comes to trial. Captain, I understand what you are saying; however, how did you get a video of the rapist engaged in a crime?"

"Andrew, I am going to show you a video made just this morning of yourself coming into this office. Now, I don't have any camera in here, agreed?"

"Agreed."

The captain had set his laptop up on the Magistrate's desk and waited while it booted up.

There, prominent on the desktop, was the video named "magistrate." The captain clicked on it and turned the computer around so the Magistrate could watch the video.

The magistrate was puzzled at first, trying to understand what he was looking at. Then he realized that he was watching himself coming in through the courthouse front door, nodding and talking to his staff, then unlocking the door to his chambers and entering. The next scene was of him making a cup of coffee and spilling some on his desk. He mopped it up with a tea towel, then sat down and took a call on his hand phone, then finished his coffee.

Then the Captain entered the chambers and took the seat offered by himself. The video came to an end.

The magistrate looked around for a camera before asking how the captain got the video when he had never been inside his chambers, and it was shot just a short time ago.

"Well, Andrew, that is a mystery that I am going to disclose to you now; however, it is for your ears only. This is one of the closest guarded secrets in the country. Do I have your word that you will keep it to yourself and not discuss it with anyone else?"

"Of course, Captain, but I am still puzzled about this video."

"I will tell you a story about a young fellow called The Time Walker."

The captain held up a hand to stop Andrew from asking any questions.

"Now, he has approved me to tell you about his discovery. He has the ability to walk back in time and see what has happened. He explained to me that he cannot see the future as that has not happened, and the present is there for everyone to see. This is like looking at the stars at night. You can see a star, but what you are looking at is the light from a million years ago. He explained to me it was part theory of Albert Einstein and part Nicola Tesla, and he has cracked the code to do this. He has become my guardian angel and my means to bring to justice criminals who have committed crimes and have thought they have gotten away with them. I cannot explain it any better than that, so I have learned to listen to what he tells me as he is always correct.

It has been his tip-offs for the buried people out on the farm, the crack house, and the rapist.

I have a video of the rapist in action, and I really don't want to show you that video, as it is horrific, and this guy needs to be locked away for a long time, which is why I need a warrant to search his unit to see what evidence is there that will help convict him when he comes to trial. I don't want him released on bail, as he will threaten the girls who have complained about him; however, it is his DNA that will convict him."

"Captain, I find this whole story amazing and so hard to comprehend, but if what you say is correct, and I have no reason to doubt you, after looking at this video, he will not be released on bail. Just keep me in the loop of what is happening about the place."

The Captain stood up, along with Andrew, who handed over the search warrant.

The captain picked up his laptop and opened the door. He looked back to see the magistrate sitting down and shaking his head.

The captain could see that the magistrate was going to have a confusing day sorting everything out in his head.

It was a lovely Autumn day as the pair walked back to the police station. The captain was in good humour as he shouldered his way through the rabble at the front door.

Even they could not take the edge off his high spirits.

The Captain walked into the ready room and handed the search warrant to the chief of detectives.

"Detective Browning, check out the accommodation of our friend down in the cells and see what you find. Take a forensic person, a camera with you, and a plainclothes officer, and let's see if he was a collector of souvenirs from his victims. I hope he was because I want to lock this slimebag away for a long, long time."

Chief Detective Browning took the warrant and collected some gear and a couple of officers and headed out.

The Captain went through to the coffee machine and made himself a double espresso and took a couple of shortbread biscuits and went into his office.

The paperwork had piled up, so he settled in for a full morning of catching up.

Work was ongoing at the "Hill Top farm and the crack house."

He worked steadily until noon and then decided it was time for a break and a trip out to the farm to check the progress on both farms.

The phone rang.

"Good morning, Captain. I see that you are catching up on your paperwork and that your men are searching the accommodation of the sleazebag rapist."

"That is correct, young fellow. What can I do for you today?"

"Well, Captain, your people have not found anything in the accommodation we were just talking about and are getting ready to come back to the police station. Give your detective a call and tell him to go downstairs and look under the staircase to the units. He will see a small door with a lock on it. This is to access the services under the units. Well, our friend has a suitcase under there which they need to bring back to the station. It contains some items of clothing that will tie our sleazebag's fingerprints to the suitcase and the clothing inside. Talk later, Captain."

The phone went dead.

The Captain promptly phoned his chief detective.

"Hello, Captain."

"Detective, under the staircase at the rear of the units, you will find a small access door with a lock on it. Inside, you will find a suitcase with the accused's fingerprints on the handle and elsewhere. Bag it and bring it back to the station. Get some good photos as well before touching it."

"Will do, Captain."

The captain hung up and sat back in his chair. Once again, the Time Walker had come through for them.

His day was going very well now, and it was time for a trip out to the farms for a look-see.

Chapter 34

VISIT TO THE CRACK HOUSE

The day got more beautiful as time went by. The trees were all changing colour, the air was crisp and clean, and the sky was a beautiful blue as he walked out to the police car park with his bodyguard. The captain was thinking of taking a few days off and going down to the coast with his wife to have a couple of days away from the full-on activity currently happening at the moment. Sergeant Timms was waiting in the patrol car, so they piled in and pushed their way through the members of the fifth estate and headed to the farm.

Thirty minutes later, they pulled up out in the country, firstly at the crack house, as the Captain thought of it.

They stood for a minute, getting their bearings and looking at the place.

"Innocent place, Sergeant. Who would believe so much death and pain emanated from here? Let's have a look now that the forensic people are nearly finished."

The bodyguard stationed himself in a patch of sunlight, as there was a little chill in the air out in the country. The Captain and the sergeant went to the front door and called the forensic people, asking if they could come inside.

"No worries, Captain, we are just packing up. We have dusted the whole place and got a lot of fingerprints. We have searched every room and looked up in the ceiling in case there was anything hidden there. We have boxed up all the chemicals and equipment for later court cases. The weapons are all locked in gun safes and ready for transport to the police station. The labs have been stripped clean, and the drugs are all boxed as evidence. We have searched every nook and cranny in the house and the farm shed."

"Well, you people have done a lot of work, so the sergeant and I will just have a wander about and have a look around if that is okay?"

"Go for it, Captain. We will start loading everything into the work van, then we will go across to the other farm and start helping out there."

The Captain wandered through the farmhouse, which was now covered in fingerprint dust, cupboards pulled apart, and clothing piled in heaps after searching.

There was still blood on the floor where the shooter had met his demise.

There was not a lot to see, so the pair went out the rear door and looked around the surroundings.

The farm buildings had all been searched, and every door to the sheds was open. Everything appeared like a normal farm; however, there was something that did not seem right to the captain. He just couldn't put a finger on it. Something was different from the norm.

They walked around the farmhouse and the farm shed, did a cursory walk through the laboratory, now stripped of all the equipment, and came back out into the Autumn sunshine.

The Captain stopped and looked about, then he turned and looked back the way they had come.

"What is it, Captain?"

"Sarge, something is not quite correct here, but I don't know what it is that is wrong. When the forensic people are finished and leave, I want two patrol officers here, and tell them to be alert until I work out what is different. Is that understood?"

"Yes, sir. I will organise it now. I have a few extra men."

"Make sure we have a couple of the Tactical Squad personnel here as well to give them a bit more firepower."

The sarge nodded but was not sure what they were guarding against.

The Captain gave the forensic people the OK to go across to the farm across the road.

The Captain slowly walked away and back to the car, thinking all the time.

They climbed into the car, and the Sarge drove them out to the road and across to "Hill Top Farm."

The fifth estate were still milling about on the road.

"They never give up, do they? Like a bunch of ghouls waiting for the dead."

When they arrived, the Captain and the others exited the vehicle, and the Captain was still thinking deeply.

"All right, let's have a talk to the forensic people."

Some of the forensic people were working in the rubbish pit and some on the other excavated grave. The forensic person called the Captain over and pointed at the bones of a human foot showing above the soil.

"That makes two from this grave site and one over there under the trees, and one out in the national park. A serial killer or killers, Captain?"

The Captain nodded. "Could still be more buried around here as well. I am going to take a walk around. You people know what to do. It is a sad duty that we all have here, but we need to ensure that these victims get a decent burial after all this time and not just be chucked in the bottom of a rubbish pit."

A nodding of heads signified that they were in agreement.

The Captain turned and walked off and, alone, started a walk around the farm in a big circle.

His phone rang.

"Hello, young fellow. What am I missing over the road?"

"Keep gnawing away at it like a dog with a bone, Captain, and if you have not cracked it by four PM, then I will give you another clue."

The phone went dead.

The Captain concentrated on the area around the farmhouse, and he knew that there were other graves there as he could feel the sadness in the air and feel the evil that had been perpetuated on young people. He kept on walking; however, the farmhouse across the road was niggling at his thoughts all the time.

Like a dog with a bone, he kept gnawing away at the puzzle. Then it hit him.

Chapter 35

THE TUNNEL

"Sergeant."

"Yes, sir."

"Get another couple of tactical response people. I know what is wrong across the road."

The four officers climbed into the armoured vehicle and drove across to the farmhouse. The forensic people were about to drive off when the captain stopped them.

"Still more work here, people. Just pull over there under that tree until I give you the word."

The Captain called everyone to come with him around the rear of the house.

"OK, we have here a dog kennel and chain, a food bowl that has never had dog food in it, and no water bowl. But where is the dog? There was no dog here when we raided the place, and I don't remember any dog in the videos taken of the place. Look at the kennel, and you can see drag marks on the ground where the dog kennel has been moved.

Sarge, is there any power being used inside the house? Fridge, hot water, anything?"

The forensic person gave a shake of his head. "Everything is turned off, Captain."

"Find the power box and tell me if the meter is still turning around, Sarge."

The Sarge was back in a moment. "Meter still turning, Captain."

"OK, that tells us that somewhere on this farm there is still power being used."

"Right, two of you check out around the kennel for wires or strings or pressure-sensitive switches."

Two officers bent over and down and checked out the dog kennel, which was hinged to the house on one side.

"Nothing, Captain."

"OK, grab that dog kennel and drag it out and away from that wall. Rest of you, have your weapons aimed at where the dog kennel is now."

The two officers grabbed the dog kennel and pulled, and the kennel swung out away from the wall, revealing a tunnel going in under the house and down into the ground.

"Torches, please."

Two torches appeared, and the tactical response people shone them down the tunnel.

Lights came on just at that moment, showing steps and a string of lights along the tunnel.

"Must have a light-sensitive switch to light up the tunnel. Right, one tactical response officer to lead with night vision goggles on just in case they can turn the power off from the other end."

The first officer started down the steps, followed by the Captain with his handgun drawn.

"Sarge, stay here and keep an eye out in case we flush anybody out into the scrub. Keep your officers here, and the second tactical officer can follow me."

The Sarge and the officers turned and started looking about the farm, which had taken on a whole new meaning since the tunnel discovery.

The Captain followed the tactical response officer, and they cautiously moved along the tunnel, watching for an ambush and any booby traps. The Captain could hear the hum of exhaust fans in the background noise.

They had not gone 10 meters when they came to a door. Everyone stopped and looked at the door, and they were all thinking booby trap.

One of the tactical officers turned to the Captain. "What do you reckon, Captain?"

"Guys, I reckon we back out of here and have a look at our options before we touch that door."

The two tactical response personnel nodded their heads and backed down the tunnel and up the stairs. They all breathed a sigh of relief being back in the open air again.

"Guys, the hairs on the back of my neck are saying stay away from that door."

Both officers nodded their heads and agreed.

Just at that moment, the Captain's phone rang.

"Hello, young fellow."

"Captain, there is no phone reception in that tunnel. Stay out of there. The exit is in the trees behind where the machine gun was set up. That's how they got the machine gun set up without us knowing that it was waiting for a raid.

The entrance is well hidden but safe to go in from that end.

There are explosives in a room in that tunnel. I would get the bomb squad up from Sydney. They are experts at this sort of setup."

"Thanks for the advice. I will chase the commissioner up when you are finished."

"Captain, it was good to see you work out the clues. You are getting better every day. Bye for now."

The commissioner came on the phone almost immediately.

"Hello, Captain. How can I help you?"

"Well, Commissioner, we have found a tunnel under the crack house, and my mate has told me the door in the tunnel is booby-trapped and we better get the bomb squad up here to disarm it. The exit is well hidden amongst the trees, but there is no booby trap on that end, so we will have a look around and see if we can find the exit, but we will wait until the bomb squad arrives to go into the tunnel and disarm the surprise, they left for us."

"That's very good advice, Captain. Just keep a guard on the place until they arrive this afternoon with all their gear."

"Thanks, sir. We will let you know what we find."

The line went dead.

The Captain shook his head.

"He never says goodbye, just hangs up on you."

"Right, Sarge. One officer to guard this entrance so no one comes out and gets away, and nobody goes in at all. The rest of you come around the front of the farmhouse and let's see if we can find the exit."

They all trooped around the end of the farmhouse and headed towards where the machine gun had been set up during the raid.

When they arrived, there was nothing obvious, and it was a typical bit of bush.

"Anybody notice anything out of the ordinary?" A half dozen pairs of eyes looked around, but nothing seemed out of the ordinary.

"Right, let's look at the vegetation and trees growing here. They are all Eucalypts except one tree. Now gum trees are hard to grow in pots and transplant because they have a tap root. Damage that tap root and they die. One tree here is not native to this area, and that is this one tree over here. A Japanese Maple, if I am not mistaken.

Let's clean around the base of the tree before we do anything else." Two sets of willing hands swept the leaves away, and there was the outline of a steel door.

"That tree was planted to help hide the entrance door.

Let's leave it at that for the time being until we have the bomb squad here."

"Right, we are not going any further until the bomb squad says it is safe to do so. However, let's get a guard on this end, the same as the other end. I don't know if we have any of our friends still down there or did we get them all the other night. That is the question, so stay alert."

That comment made everyone look at the trap door with a different viewpoint than a few minutes ago.

"Forensic, let's get the drugs and weapons and anything else into town and locked up. Myself and my tactical person will escort you to the station. Sarge, you keep an eye on the two farms and I will escort the bomb squad out here when they arrive."

"Will do, Captain."

There was a shuffling of people, and then the vehicles went back across the road to the other farm, and the Forensic van and the Captain's vehicle headed off into town and the police station.

The Captain spoke to the Forensic people to exhibit the drugs, weapons, and other relevant equipment on the concrete back landing of the police station.

"Call me when it is laid out, and we will get the TV crews out for some shots before we lock it all away. I also want two Tactical response people and two uniformed officers on guard the whole time so we can control the horde from dipping their fingers into any of the booty, so to speak."

"Yes, sir, I will call you when it is all laid out. Do you want to include the weapons from your shootout the other night?"

"Yes, everything. Cover it all with a light tarpaulin so they all get to see it at the same time. Show them that we are not just country hicks."

Chapter 36

EXPOSURE TO THE PRESS

An hour later, there was a knock at the Captain's door.

"All ready, Captain."

"Right, Constable Wilkins, please go out to the front and invite the rabble around to the rear deck in an orderly manner."

"Right, Captain."

The Captain and two forensic, two detectives, and two uniformed members went outside and stood behind the display.

The press filed around the corner and stood in front of the tarpaulin. TV cameras hummed, and presenters spoke quietly into their microphones.

"Good morning, all. I am Captain Wilson, and I have invited the press into our compound to view some of the weapons, drugs, and apparatus that we have removed from the farm drug manufacturing facility that we raided the other evening. Please remove the tarpaulin, officers."

The tarpaulin was whisked off like a magician at a party, and the full extent of the captured goods was exposed.

The machine gun and the rocket-propelled grenade were prominent in the front, ahead of the Uzi submachine pistols and handguns. There were boxes of packaged drugs, sacks of money neatly tied into bundles, and boxes of ammunition.

"This organization was not a backyard affair to make some drugs for their personal use. It was a well-planned, well-equipped, and well-armed operation, and my teams have done a great job busting up this manufacturing facility without any loss of life.

We have also found a tunnel under the farmhouse that has a booby-trapped entrance, and we are currently waiting on the bomb squad to arrive to dismantle any nasty surprises that they have left behind. Now, any questions?"

The noise started immediately until the Captain held up his hand, then they all went silent.

"You, sir, what is your question?"

"Captain, where did these people get a machine gun and RPG from?"

"That is something that we are investigating at this time. Next question. You, young lady."

"Where were the drugs going to, and have those people been arrested?"

"Drugs were going to outlets in the Sydney area, and there were drug raids on suspected outlets in Sydney at the same time as the drug raid on the farmhouse, so that question needs to be directed to senior staff in Sydney."

"Are there any other drug manufacturing places in this area?"

"We are studying all the information we have been able to gather from the farmhouse, and when we have collated it all, we will know more about the drug organization and what other locations they might have."

"Please feel free to photograph what is on display, then all of this will be locked in our evidence vault until it is no longer needed, and then the drugs will be destroyed.

You have a further ten minutes, then we would ask you to please clear the compound in an orderly manner. Thank you."

The Captain turned and spoke to his staff. "Watch them like a hawk so they don't pinch anything, then turf them out on the street again."

"Aye, aye, Captain."

The Captain went back inside and headed for the urn to make a cup of tea.

The inevitable paperwork drew him to his office, and he sat down and started catching up on the reports. He often wondered, did anyone ever read them when they made their way to head office? Still, it was all part of the job.

It was late afternoon when Constable Wilkins brought an officer into his office and knocked on his door.

"Come in."

"Captain, the officer in charge of the bomb squad, Senior Sergeant O'Brian, please meet Captain Wilson."

The Captain stood and shook hands. "Pleased to meet you. Would you like a tea or coffee?"

"No thanks, Captain. Give us a rundown on the job you have for us. I understand that you people have just had a drug bust here that has made national headlines."

"Well, Sergeant, we have been given a tip-off that the tunnel that we found has been booby-trapped at the entrance under the dog kennel; however, we were told that there are no booby traps from the outlet end of the tunnel. Just like the drug raid, we wanted some expert people to check it all out, hence you being here. We are grateful to have your expertise, as I don't want anybody being hurt on my watch. It is getting towards dark, so do you want to have a look now or wait until tomorrow morning?"

"Captain, I would like a look, but we will not attempt anything until we have good daylight, so if we could just have a look-see now, it would be appreciated."

"Constable Wilkins, could you take the Senior Sergeant for a run out to the farm so they can have a look before dark? I will ring the sergeant and ensure that we have some guards on the farm overnight."

"No problems, sir. Would you come through, Sergeant?"

They both left, and the Captain went back to his thankless task of writing reports about the previous events of the last week.

The Captain took a wander around the station and found that all the guns and evidence had been locked away. The prisoners from the drug raid were all gone to the remand centre.

The detectives who had searched the alleged rapist's accommodation and found the suitcase were in the squad room, catching up on paperwork as well.

"Chief detective, what did you find in the suitcase?"

"Well, Captain, like you suspected, he was a souvenir keeper, which will ensure we can tie him to the other rapes as well. Forensic has lifted his fingerprints from the suitcase, and inside there were bras and panties, and we are sure that the lab will find his semen and hairs on some of the items.

We will get the victims to come and identify their articles of clothing before we charge him with multiple rapes and assaults."

"When he was wandering down the street with his coffee this morning, I bet he never thought his day would end with himself in gaol and facing a bleak future."

"Good work, all of you. This will clean up some cold cases as well as bring justice to a lot of people who had given up hope of their assailant ever being caught."

The Captain looked at the time and decided it was time to go home during daylight for once, so he gathered his gear and headed home with his bodyguard.

Sitting in the pergola with a cold beer and some cheese and sausage, he was joined by his wife.

"Well, Bill, this makes for a nice change to the evenings than earlier this last week."

"Mavis, I was thinking we might go down the coast for a couple of days to your family beach house this weekend if you want."

"Bill, darling, that would be nice."

"Well, the sergeant and the chief detective can handle the place for a few days if you want to make the arrangements and pack a couple of bags. I still have fishing gear down there, and a bit of fishing from the beach would be nice."

Night fell on another day for the Captain and the Time Walker.

The Captain was down at the police station next morning by 6:30 am.

The bomb squad was there, all meeting the sergeant, who was an old mate.

Coffee was flowing freely, and the Captain had a cup and joined in the chatter until five to seven, when he called out, "OK, everyone, a quick meeting on where we are at the moment."

"Chief of detectives, what's the word on the owners of the farm?"

"Nothing yet, sir. The Lands department is dragging the chain. I rang them yesterday and they promised me that they would have the information in a few days."

"OK, have you been in touch with your mate in the Federal Police regarding the machine gun and RPG?"

"Yes, Captain, I gave him the serial numbers and he is looking into it, and I will probably need to take a visit to Canberra to accompany him to the Army Headquarters, as they are not being very helpful. We expected them to push back, and that is what they are doing, so we will need to threaten a few of them with arrest. However, that would need to come from the Federal Police, as we have no jurisdiction on Federal land."

"Forensic, what is the status on the DNA from the first victim we found in the national park and the two families who have lost loved ones here in town?"

"Well, Captain, they are progressing as quickly as possible, but DNA testing is a slow process.

We now have the sleazebag rapist and the victim's clothes from the suitcase, as well as other lots of DNA to do, so we will keep pressure on the lab, but it is a case of slowly, slowly, at this time."

"Have we been able to identify all of the prisoners from the crack house?"

"Fingerprints have identified all the people who were killed, as they all had criminal records. However, the laboratory chemists and the helpers are more difficult, as most of them don't speak English and most of them don't have any paperwork or IDs."

"Well, keep at it and get a social worker from Sydney for the language barrier. They will do gaol time then be deported back to their home countries. I know all the bleeding hearts will be saying they had no other work and they are innocent, but they knew what they were doing was illegal."

"Forensic, how is the exhuming of the deceased at the farm going?"

"We will be finished with the three that we have uncovered this afternoon. Then we will go searching with the ground-penetrating radar for more bodies."

"Now, as these are dating back years, there will be trees growing over the site of the bodies as the blood and bone makes for good fertilizer, so check around close to every tree and not just the clear areas between the trees. A lot of these trees would have only grown in the last years since the victims were buried."

"Any questions? No. OK, we will take the bomb boys and ladies out to the farm, so stay away from the crack house until we give everyone the clear signal."

"Thank you all for your great help the past week."

Chapter 37

THE BOMB SQUAD

The meeting broke up and people streamed out the rear door to their patrol cars, and the bomb squad lingered for a moment to have a word with the Captain.

"Come into my office, Senior Sergeant. Bring your coffee with you. Take a seat.Now, how can we be of assistance as your line of work is different from what we normally do?"

"Well, Captain, we are pretty well self-contained and what we will do is remotely open the door to the tunnel just in case they have some sort of trigger on it. Then we will search the underground bunker and find out just what they were doing down there. What we find will determine our next steps—either disarm any ordnance or explode it in situ."

"Well, if you need anything at all, you call the sergeant and we will be only too happy to assist. I will be out there myself in an hour, but please be careful."

"Always, Captain. We will be on our way."

They all took their leave, and the squad room was almost empty. Just the odd person writing a report.

"Chief detective, a moment please?"

"Yes, sir."

"I am thinking of going away for a couple of days this coming weekend. I would like you to take charge while I am away. I don't expect any issues as things should quieten down now as we go into the prosecution stage of these crimes."

"No worries, Captain. It has been a very hectic time, that's for sure."

"Much appreciated. Now I want to go out to the crack house and see how the bomb squad is going."

The Captain walked out to the front desk and asked the constable if she could get a replacement so she could drive him out to the crack house.

"No worries, Captain. Just make yourself a takeaway coffee and I will get a replacement for the front desk, and we can take the van again as it has had a new windscreen fitted. Still got a few dings in the front, but all safe to drive. I will be out the back in a few minutes."

The Captain took the constable's advice, made himself a takeaway long flat white, and wandered out to stand in the sun along with his bodyguard.

"I think you might be redundant after today, Mr. Bodyguard."

"You will need to talk to my boss about that, Captain. They don't want to lose you and I enjoy the different work."

The constable arrived with the van keys and they all piled in and headed out to the street.

"Well, the news must be quiet in other parts of Australia as the crowd outside the police station has not gotten any less."

Forty minutes later, after a pleasant drive through the countryside, they arrived at the crack house. The Captain and his entourage all got out and waited for the sergeant from the Bomb Squad to come to them.

A few minutes later, they were joined by the sergeant in charge.

"How is it all going, sergeant?"

"Well, Captain, there were no booby traps this end of the tunnel, but you were correct about the door down the other end. It was wired up, so if you had opened it, you would be waiting at the pearly gates for them to let you in."

"Did you get some photos, Sergeant, of the booby trap?"

"Yes, Captain. We will also use them in our instructions to new recruits. Very ingenious and very deadly. You guys did the right thing leaving the door alone. Now, come down here one at a time and have a look at how busy these guys were."

The Captain followed the bomb squad leader across to the hidden door and down the staircase. The tunnel was lit by a string of lights, and then they were inside a large room which was well-lit as well.

"Captain, I believe these guys were manufacturing explosive devices here, so we have asked for an expert to come up from Sydney to give the place the once-over. We have dismantled and removed any booby traps, so everything in here is safe to touch. However, I would get forensic down here first to fingerprint the place as we might have the culprits on record."

The Captain was astounded by the size of the room. "It is so much bigger than what I thought it would be."

"Captain, I think it might have been a commercial wine cellar at one time and they expanded it and dug some escape tunnels as well. There is also a ladder going up into the house with a very well-hidden trap door in the floor. You would not see it from above, but when you push up the floor, it becomes obvious."

The Captain was truly astounded by the size of the underground room and the amount of chemical apparatus set up in the place.

"Well, I look forward to hearing from the expert about what they were doing down here. If they were using the farm shed for manufacturing drugs, why have they got this setup here in the cellar, and they appear to have air extraction fans as well?"

The Captain had a good look around and then exited the cellar through the dog kennel door.

He walked around to the front entrance and surprised everyone who were looking down the stairs into the cellar.

"One at a time if you want to have a look, but don't touch anything as we need to get forensic back over here and down there to fingerprint every last piece of equipment and see if we can get a match with anyone in our database."

The constable was away first, and the Captain stood in the autumn sunshine, enjoying the peace and quiet of the countryside after the hurly-burly of the police station.

The constable was soon back with them.

"Captain, I am astounded at the size of the place."

"Go on, bodyguard, go and have a look at what the crims had going for them here, which is why they did not want to give the place up."

"Are you sure, Captain?" looking about as if they were going to be attacked at any moment.

"The constable and I are both armed and you won't be gone more than a few minutes."

The bodyguard was back under 5 minutes and seemed relieved that the Captain was still in one piece.

"Big Captain. What were they doing down there?"

"That, young fellow, is the 64,000-dollar question that we have to find the answer to."

Chapter 38

MORE GRAVES

They all climbed back into the van and headed across to the other farm.

The constable had to blow the horn and hit the siren to get the press to move away to allow the van access to the farm.

When they stopped and exited the van, they could see the forensic team with the ground-penetrating radar working among the trees.

The Captain caught up with the head of forensic, and before he could say a word, the officer nodded his head.

"You were right, Captain; these trees have been planted, and we have discovered what appears to be another grave under a tree."

"Right, show me, where."

The pair walked over, and the captain nodded his head.

"I can feel the person's buried here crying out for justice. Treat the remains with respect and be very thorough in your searching, as we don't want to miss anybody. They have been together for many years, and they need to all go out of here together."

"Yes, Captain. I will get the backhoe started, knock down the tree, and start excavating."

The Captain walked away back to the van, and along the way, his phone rang.

He glanced at the number.

"Hello, young fellow. We have just found another set of remains. How many more?"

"Captain, firstly well done on finding the cellar, and I am not sure what they were manufacturing there. Next, I have been spending a lot of time looking at the farm where you are going back to the days when it held a young family and there was laughter about the place. I believe that you will find three more sets of remains, and that will be all here on the farm. These evil people did not bury their victims anywhere else, with the one exception of the young lady in the national park. Take your good lady and take a few days off and go fishing down the coast. You have a good team of people here who will look after things while you are away. I will keep an eye on things here and on you down at the beach. Give my regards to your wife. Goodbye."

The Captain walked back to the van, where the constable was waiting.

"Did they find another victim, Captain?"

"Aye, they did, and my young mate tells me that there are three more to be found after this one, and that is all that have been buried by the same people."

"Captain, go home and pack up and go away like you were thinking about. Everyone here can look after what is happening. Get some fresh salt air and catch a fish or two."

"Thank you, Constable, that is good advice. Let's go back to town and face the horde, and I will ring the commissioner and let him know what is going on around here."

The three of them piled into the van and headed back to town.

"Constable, stop at the gate, and I will give the press some news to shut them up. I don't want them driving the chief detective and the Sergeant insane with their questions."

"Yes, sir, however, they are like a pack of hungry sharks. Never sated by the news you give them, they want more all the time, and when they don't get any more, they start talking rubbish over and over again."

"Such is the price we pay for living in a free country, Constable."

The Captain phoned the commissioner, who answered with his usual prompt efficiency.

"Good morning, Captain. What have you got for me today?"

"Sir, the bomb squad has cleared all the booby traps from the underground room, which looks like it used to be a wine cellar and they expanded it. The forensic team are searching the other farm for more graves, and they believe they have found another burial site. My young friend said that there are three more souls buried there yet to be discovered."

"Bloody hell, Captain, this area you have out there is really in the news. Right, tell the press what you have found, and Captain, take a few days off to revive your spirits."

With that, the phone went dead.

"He never ever says goodbye. No. I tell a lie. One day he did say goodbye."

The van stopped short of the police guard, and the Captain got out and walked up to the officer on duty.

"Walk with me to the lion's den, young fellow, so I can give them some news."

The young constable did not seem too happy with that instruction; however, he walked with the Captain and his bodyguard.

They stopped three meters short of the nearest press, and the Captain called out.

"Good morning, all."

There were mumbled good mornings back.

"Right, some news for your followers. We have discovered an underground laboratory at the crack farm where we did the drug bust the other night. We believe that it was originally a wine cellar that they expanded and were using for their illegal activities. This cellar had two exits and a hidden entrance inside the house so they could access the cellar without going outside the farmhouse. One entrance was booby-trapped so that anybody opening the most obvious door would have been blown apart. We have some technical chemists coming from Sydney to study the place to see if we can discover what they were making in the cellar. The farm across the road, where we are standing outside of now, has already yielded three sets of remains, and our people using ground-penetrating radar believe they have found another grave site, which they will start to excavate later today. In total, to date, we have found four sets of remains of their victims, and all those remains have been sent to the main laboratory in Sydney. It is hoped that we can get identification of those remains through DNA and dental records. Now, any intelligent questions?"

The press seemed at a loss for a moment, then a hand went up.

"Captain, do you expect to find any other remains on the farm after this victim?"

"I can't answer that. I would hope not, however, we are not leaving here until I am certain that there is nobody else calling for justice from their graves."

Everything went quiet again, so the Captain turned and went back to the van.

"Thank you, Constable. That was not that bad, was it?"

"No, sir. They seem to be in a daze at the moment."

The captain climbed back into the van, as did the bodyguard.

"All right, Constable, drive us to town and no detours down road embankments this time."

This was said with a chuckle. The Constable's only comment was, "I'll try, sir, just for you."

The trip this time was uneventful and enjoyable in the autumn weather. The trees were all going from green to yellow to red, the air was crisp and clean, and the sky was a beautiful blue with just a few high cirrus clouds.

They pulled into the rear of the police station and exited the van.

"Constable, give me half an hour and then you might like to drive me home as I might get away a bit early today. It's a great day for a run in the convertible."

They all went into the squad room where they split up to go to their respective work areas.

"Captain, there is a gentleman outside who would like to speak to you."

"Who is it, constable?"

"A Mr. Atkins, sir."

"I wondered when he would turn up. Bring him through, and please stay as a witness to the conversation."

"Yes, sir."

A few minutes later, the constable showed an elderly gentleman into the Captain's office.

He was well-dressed and had a head of grey hair.

The Captain stood up and introduced himself. "Captain Wilson. Pleased to meet you, Mr. Atkins. How may I help you? Please be seated."

The old gentleman seated himself and seemed to be at a loss for words.

Finally, he gathered himself and asked the question. "I understand that you have my son in gaol at the moment. Could you please tell me what he is charged with? I have been away for a while and just returned this morning, which is why I have not been down here earlier."

"Mr. Atkins, it is my sad duty to inform you that we have arrested your son for armed assault, firstly as he threatened Maureen with a knife. Secondly, we are doing tests at this time, which will tie him to multiple cases of rape and assault around the district."

The old man looked like somebody had bludgeoned him with a heavy stick.

"My God, he has gone too far this time, and he will have to face the future by himself, whatever that may be. I am not going to try and get him off any charges that you bring. He is such a disappointment to his late mother and myself."

"I am sorry that this has happened, Mr. Atkins. However, he has done some brutal assaults to young ladies and up to now has been able to escape justice, but it has all caught up with him."

The old gentleman stood up and reached for the Captain's hand. "You must ensure, Captain, that he pays for his sins and the young ladies get justice. I am sorry that this has happened. His mother would turn in her grave if she knew what he has done. Thank you."

He turned and walked out. The constable followed him out of the police station and asked if he was going to be all right driving.

"Yes, thank you, Constable. I will go to the office and see Maureen. Thank you."

The constable went back in to see the Captain.

"There is another parent who feels they are responsible for their children's sins."

"Maureen said he was a real gentleman."

"Take me back to my place, constable, and I will get away early for the coast. I have a nice rod and Alvey side-cast reel that was my grandfather's, and I can feel the fish biting already."

"C'mon, Captain, I will have you home in ten minutes."

The constable was as true as her word.

Chapter 39

DAY AT THE BEACH

The Captain called out to his wife. "I am home, darling. How far are we away from being packed?"

"Everything is ready; I just want to know what car we are taking."

"Well, the weather forecast is for fine, sunny weather, so we will take my car and give it a good run."

The Captain started carrying a couple of small suitcases down to the garage and came back for some boxes of food.

He took the keys from the key rack and went down to the garage, firing up the '67 Ford Mustang that the Captain had had for many years—his pride and joy. The rumble of the 289 cubic inch small block V8 engine made him think he was 19 again.

Fifteen minutes later, they were pulling away from the house with a wave to his next-door neighbour, Bob.

The top was down, and the pair of them enjoyed the drive over the Blue Mountains and down to the coast. They hit the North-South highway and turned North.

An hour later, they pulled into the driveway of the family beach house in a small coastal village some miles away from the main Pacific highway. Thirty minutes later, everything was stowed away in the beach house, and they were sitting on the front deck looking out across the ocean, which had just some small waves coming ashore.

There were some hopeful surfers sitting on their boards looking out to sea, but they were bound to be disappointed, waiting for a decent wave.

The Captain was wearing a pair of board shorts, an old T-shirt, and a Bunnings straw hat. He was working on making a couple of lures so he could get down to the beach just before the sun came up and do some beach fishing. It had been a while, but it was like riding a bicycle—you never forgot how.

It was soon turning twilight, and the Captain lit the deck barbecue and threw on two steaks and some prawns while his wife made a salad. They were soon enjoying a nice meal with candles burning on the table and a bottle of Merlot being shared.

They were soon inside, sleeping the sleep of the innocent.

The Captain padded down the stairs in the predawn light with his rod and his Alvey side-cast reel and his new lures. Ten minutes later, he made his first cast out into the ocean, which was as still as a millpond. Nothing—not a nibble on the lure—so he moved along the beach, looking for the gutters that would mean there were fish lurking there, waiting for a meal to come swimming past or a lure to head for the shore.

He was soon joined by another fisherman, a younger man who was using live bait that he had in a bucket. They nodded to each other, and the pair kept moving along the beach, casting and reeling in their lures and live bait.

The Captain's phone rang in his pocket. Force of habit had made him put his phone in his pocket.

He pulled it out and saw it was from his young mate, the Time Walker.

"Good morning, young fellow."

"Captain, there is a young lady who has been buried alive just behind you in the sand dunes and needs your help urgently. Grab that bait bucket from the other fisher so you can dig her out. Hurry, you do not have much time."

The Captain hurled his rod up the beach and sprinted across to the other fisherman. He grabbed his bait bucket and tipped everything in it out onto the beach.

The fisherman was stunned and could not believe what was happening.

"I am a police Captain. Come with me now. We need to save a young girl's life. Don't ask questions, just come."

The Captain ran along the beach with the phone to his ear.

"Stop, Captain, and turn right and go up into the sand dunes. Hurry. Jump the environmental fence and climb the sand dune. Over the top and down to the bottom." The Captain heard the other fisherman behind him.

"Stop now, Captain. Start digging right in front of you. Hurry."

"Mate, if this is some sort of joke, I will belt the daylights out of you." This was said in the Captain's ear.

"Shut up and dig with this bucket while I dig with my hands. Hurry, or we will be too late."

Not a word was said for the next couple of minutes—just the panting of the two fishermen.

Suddenly, they hit some newspaper, and the Captain swept the last of the sand off of it and lifted the paper out of the hole they had dug. Human hair was exposed, and then a face. The Captain handed the phone to the fisherman and said, "Ring for an ambulance with two paramedics and then call the police."

The Captain felt around the girl's neck. "She is still alive," as he bent down and started giving her a few breaths to help her breathing.

By this time, their activity had attracted other early morning beachgoers who came over to see what was happening.

"Don't stand there gawking; get digging. Get some weight off her chest to make it easier for her to breathe."

The young people got in with a will and were digging like crazy. Six young people were pulling the sand off of her buried body while the Captain gave her extra breaths. Her heart was still beating slowly. Other arrivals started pulling the excavated sand away from the first people who started digging.

"Somebody get up to the road so the ambulance knows where to stop. Tell the paramedics that they should bring a bottle of oxygen and a face mask down here to where we are."

"Did you ring the police as well?"

"Yes, Captain, they will be here in a few minutes with shovels as well."

The Captain could hear the sirens of the ambulance and police coming, but he did not let anybody stop.

"Keep digging. If you are tired, swap with somebody who has not had a go at digging her out." When the Captain gave an order, they all listened.

People swapped positions, and the digging continued. The Captain continued giving the girl breaths to assist her breathing.

Next moment, there was a paramedic there with a face mask.

"Right, mate, let me get this on her."

The Captain was exhausted and fell backward onto the sand.

"You okay, mate?" It was the other fisherman.

"Yeah. Just getting a bit long in the tooth for this sort of exercise."

Next moment, there were two police with shovels digging like crazy.

In a few minutes, the paramedic had the girl on a stretcher, and the police and the medics took a handle each and carried her up over the dune to the boardwalk, then away to the ambulance.

They worked on stabilizing her condition for ten minutes with some injections and cleaning out any sand from her nose and mouth.

Next moment, the paramedics climbed into the ambulance, and the doors slammed, and the ambulance was away to the nearest hospital.

The police senior constable came and sat down beside the two fishermen, who were recovering on the wooden boardwalk that crossed the dunes to the beach.

"Right, first question. What the hell happened here?"

The other fisherman spoke first.

"Mate, you had better ask this guy who told me he was a police Captain and to follow him, as there was a girl who needed our help."

"So, you are the one who started the rescue, is that correct?"

The Captain nodded.

"Do you have any ID on you?"

"No, constable, but I do have it back at the beach house."

He looked at the other fisherman.

"I suppose you don't have any either, sir?"

"I drove down to the beach, officer, so here is my driver's license."

The constable took the license and compared the photo ID to the person sitting there.

"Is this address still current?"

This was answered with a nod of the head.

The fisherman looked at the Captain.

"Mate, I thought that you had gone crazy, and I was not much better following you, but it feels good that we were able to save her."

"Thanks for your help. I hope to catch up with you again on the beach."

The police officer had made a note of the name and address and license number of the fisherman.

"Where are you staying here in town, sir?"

"Ocean View Holiday Cottages, sir."

"How much longer are you booked in there for, sir?"

"Mid next week, officer. We only arrived last evening."

"Okay, sir, you may go back to your fishing. Thank you very much for your assistance in this matter. We will be in touch if we need you."

The fisherman leaned over and handed the phone back to the Captain.

"You might need this, mate." Then he was gone back to the beach after collecting his bait bucket.

"Now, back to you, Captain, if that is how you wish to be addressed. Where are you staying?"

"Last house on the beachfront. The white stucco house with the deck facing the ocean."

"Right, Captain," said with a bit of sarcasm. "Let's go down there and get your ID so I know just who I am talking to."

"OK, Senior Constable, but let's walk along the beach so I can pick up my grandfather's rod and reel if it is still there."

"OK. Bit late to seal the area off, but you never know what forensic will find." He called out to one of the other officers who was now on the scene. "Run some police tape around the whole area. I am going for a walk along the beach with the Captain here. When you get done, come down to the last house on the beachfront."

"Right, Captain, let's go for a brisk morning walk along the beach."

They both stood up and climbed onto the boardwalk and dusted any loose sand off their legs.

They walked in silence for ten minutes until they came to the Captain's rod and reel. The line had been reeled in, and the rod had been stood upright in the loose sand.

"This your rod and reel, Captain?" The Captain was again addressed with a slight note of sarcasm.

"Yes, Constable. My grandfather used to come down the coast every year and fish for Taylor when they were running. I don't get the chance very often to come fishing these days. Life seems to have gotten a lot more hectic."

"Now tell me. This is where you were fishing when you suddenly got the urge to abandon your rod and run along the beach and up into the dunes and start digging with the help of the other fisherman who you ordered to come with you. You were able to go to the precise spot where her head was and expose her, then give her assistance breathing?"

"That's correct, Constable."

"Sounds like a lot of bull dust to me, Captain. Sounds like a guilty conscience to me, but I will give you the benefit of the doubt for the moment. Let's keep walking, with you just in front of me if you don't mind."

They soon arrived at the Captain's beach house where he and his wife were staying.

He leaned the rod against the wall at the bottom of the steps and started up the stairs to the patio.

"Captain, stop for a moment." The Captain did so as the constable knocked loudly on the wall of the house.

It was only a minute or so before the Captain's wife opened the front door and looked out.

"Hello, darling. I have the coffee pot on. I see you found one of your police friends. The coffee will be ready in a minute."

"Darling, I did not catch any fish, so two plates of bacon and eggs, with baked beans, a hash brown, and toast would be lovely. Please bring my computer bag out to the patio first, love. I am covered in loose sand and don't want to track it through the house."

His wife was back in a moment with the computer bag.

"Well, come on up and sit down. The coffee will be out in a minute."

"Come on, Constable, no use standing down here by yourself. The wife makes a good cup of coffee too."

The constable came up the stairs onto the patio and took the chair indicated by the Captain. He removed his police cap. This did not appear to be going the way he thought it would. The Captain zipped the side pocket open and pulled out his police badge and ID. He handed both to the constable, who examined them.

"Are you the Captain from out west who has found all those bodies from the serial killer and had a shootout with some drive-by killers and just done a drug bust?"

"Yes, Constable. We are having a couple of days down here to recharge the batteries."

"Captain, I am sorry about my disbelieving you, but it all sounded so fanciful. I better get going back to the station."

"Not yet, Constable. First, we have breakfast, then you and I and the police commissioner need to have a talk."

The constable could see a transfer to somewhere out back of woop, woop, in his future.

"Nothing serious, Constable, and no, you will not be transferred."

The coffee arrived steaming hot. "Breakfast will be another five minutes, love."

The Captain poured two mugs out, added cream and sugar, and sat back. He indicated the coffee pot. "Get it while it is hot, mate."

Just then, the Captain's phone rang.

"Hello, young fellow. We got to her in time, but whether she will recover or not, I don't know."

"She is doing alright, Captain. I have sent you a couple of photos of the two young men who buried her not long before dawn. They are locals and live not far from where you are sitting now. Show the constable the photos. I am sure he will know them. Thank you, Captain, you have done very well today and saved a young life. Have a nice day."

The Captain booted up his computer between sips of coffee. The constable was feeling very uncomfortable drinking his coffee.

The Captain's wife arrived at that moment and placed two plates down, along with knives and forks and a plate of toast. "Who was on the phone, darling? Was it work?"

"No, it was the young fellow."

"I hope everything is OK."

"All good, love."

"Come on, Constable, dig in before it gets cold, and while you are eating, have a look at these couple of photos."

The constable started to cut into the bacon and eggs.

"Do you know these young men, Constable?"

The Captain was eating with healthy gusto.

The constable, between mouthfuls, studied the photos.

"Yes, Captain. A couple of the local surfers who live in a big house not far from where we were digging earlier."

"Right, you might go down there after breakfast and arrest them and check out their van for evidence. The blond-headed one is an accomplice; the dark-haired one was the main culprit. Call your constable up and have him photograph these men and have him go there now before they pack up and do a runner."

The constable stood up and called his two other officers who had arrived a few minutes ago.

They came up the stairs to talk to the senior constable.

"Take a photo of these two blokes and go and arrest them at the surfer house down near the boardwalk. Give me a call on my phone as soon as you have them and impound their van as well."

Photos were taken of the Captain's computer, and the two officers disappeared.

"Now sit down, Senior Constable, and finish your breakfast while I tell you what is going to happen here."

"Well, Senior Constable, how was the coffee and breakfast?"

"Good, sir."

"Right, let's go check out the accused down the road."

"Sir, I don't have a vehicle here, and it is a couple of kilometres to the surfer house."

"Well, Constable, you are about to have a treat. Darling, please give me the keys to the Mustang. I need to drop the Senior Constable off at work."

His wife came out with his keys, and the two police officers stood up.

"Thank you, ma'am, for the coffee and breakfast. It was very nice."

"I hope we see you again, Constable. Always nice to meet another officer."

The Captain led the way downstairs and pressed the button for the roller door.

The Mustang stood there gleaming, waiting for the key to turn.

"Jump in, Senior Constable, and put on your seatbelt.

The motor rumbled into life, and the Captain backed out onto the street. With a blatt on the throttle, they were away down the road towards the surfer house.

The day was perfect, and the ride was over before it began.

They parked a couple of houses away from the police vehicles. The pair climbed out and walked down towards the surfer house, followed by the stares of the curious neighbours and the stunned police officers.

"Well, Constable, have you got the two suspects in custody?"

The constable nodded. "Tell the Captain what has happened."

"Yes, sir. We arrived just as the two of them were packing their gear in the van. Both have been handcuffed and taken back to the station for questioning."

"Right, keep them separate for the time being and have their gear and the van taken to the police compound. Get onto forensic and get them fingerprinted and swabbed for drugs and DNA. Have forensic go through the van and get it fingerprinted as well. Get forensic to go to the hospital and get the young lady's fingerprints and a DNA sample. I think you will find they used the van last night."

"Yes, sir."

"Senior Constable, you men seem to have everything under control, so we might as well go to the police station as well so we can ring the commissioner."

This was something that the senior constable was not looking forward to at all.

"Come on, Senior Constable. Don't you like my Mustang?"

They were soon seated and belted in, and the motor rumbled into life. The Captain U-turned and drove off down the street, followed by a lot of sets of eyes from neighbours and tenants from the surfer house.

They were soon parked in the police car park, and the Captain indicated for the senior constable to lead the way to his office.

Heads all turned when they walked through the squad room and went into the senior's office.

Police looked at one another, shrugged their shoulders, and shook their heads.

"Right, a quick call to the commissioner."

As always, the commissioner answered almost immediately.

"Good morning, Captain. How are the fish biting?"

"Bit of drama this morning, Commissioner. My young friend called me to an emergency right next to where I was fishing. A young lady was buried alive, and myself and another fisherman, along with some early morning surfers, were able to dig her out. The paramedics and the local uniform branch also arrived with shovels, and we got her to the hospital still alive. The culprits have been arrested and are on their way to the station now."

"You never stop, do you, Captain? But well done to everyone."

"The problem now, Commissioner, is the press will get wind of this, and that will mean more questions."

"Yes. I see that as a problem as well. What do you suggest?"

"Commissioner, I think a little white lie—that the other fisherman saw a dog digging in the sand, and he went to investigate and discovered the girl—might cover the problem."

"Right, Captain. Have all the people involved send their written reports directly to me. If there are any problems, I will squash them real quick. I know nobody wants that vacant position at Woop Woop."

"Thanks, Commissioner."

"Thank you, Captain. Goodbye."

The Captain was stunned.

"Is everything OK, Captain?"

"That is the first time the commissioner has ever said goodbye. He usually just hangs up on me. This is almost cause for a celebration."

"Well, Senior Constable, you heard the commissioner. Get that other fisherman and turn him into a hero, but no mention of me at all. We have too much riding on me not being identified. I was just happy to be able to help dig her out. Is that all understood? Make sure the other fisherman knows not to mention me at all. A dog was digging and barking, but it ran away when everyone turned up."

"Yes, Captain, I will make it happen, and thank you very much for your assistance."

"Right, I might go back to the beach house and take my good wife for a drive around the area so we can see what changes have happened since we were last here. Have a good day."

With that, the Captain walked through the squad room and climbed into the Mustang, letting the rumble of the V8 take him back in time to when he first hocked his soul to buy the American muscle car.

The weather was perfect for the next two days, with the Captain catching fish early in the morning. He and the same fisherman walked the length of the beach in silence, casting and reeling in until the sun got too high in the sky and the fishing dropped off.

Back to the beach house. Clean the fish, then a quick shower, then he and his wife played tourist with visits to the local coffee shops for breakfast, then wandered through the local antique shop and bric-a-brac shops. They also took a run along the coast to the next town and did the same things there as well. Before they knew it, it was Monday lunchtime, and time to pack the Mustang and head home, ready for work on the morrow.

The Captain took one last walk down to the beach just in front of the beach house. To get to the beach, there was a flight of wooden stairs leading from the street and a bench at the bottom, which was vacant this late in the day. He sat down and looked along the beach and out to sea, thinking that he would miss this back over the mountains when his phone rang.

"Good day, young fellow."

"Good day, Captain. I know you will be happy to hear that the young lady that you assisted in saving is sitting up in bed and talking to the staff."

"Yes, I am happy to hear that. I have been wondering how she was still alive when we got her out."

"Funny you should say that, Captain. So was I, so I investigated further. It was a combination of a lot of things and some luck as well."

"Well, don't keep me in suspense, young fellow. Tell me before I have to leave and go back out west to a lot of crimes we have to solve."

"All right, Captain. Firstly, she ended up like she was because she and her boyfriend were playing sex games of choking her till she was on the verge of passing out when she was having an orgasm. However, he went a little too far, and she has an extraordinary heart, which went into shutdown mode and started beating just a few beats a minute.

The next thing he finds, she is unresponsive and can't find a pulse, so he thinks she is dead. He gets his mate, and they take her down to the sand dunes and bury her. The boyfriend can't bear the thought of sand covering her face, so he covers her face with the newspaper that the police now have with his fingerprints on. This newspaper formed an air void over her nose, and when they covered her, her head was the closest to the surface. The sand there is coarser than the rest of the beach— more like a fine dry pebble, which had a lot of air voids as well, if you remember. So, like people who fall into ice water, her body was in a preservation state. You and the fisherman arrived not long after they left and started digging her out. The paramedics did a great job of keeping her alive until she arrived at the hospital, then the hospital staff did a great job of bringing her back from the long walk over the rainbow bridge. So, all's well that ends well."

"Young fellow, it all sounds good. However, now the legal profession starts going to work. Accessory after the fact, attempted manslaughter, and other charges that the crown prosecutor will think up. Every action has an opposite reaction when it comes to doing things that border on the illegal."

"Now, don't be depressed, Captain. Jump into that Mustang and enjoy the autumn sunshine on the way home."

"I think I am just getting old, young fellow."

"Captain, you are only fifty. Still a young man."

"Time and tide wait for no man, my young friend."

"Come on, Captain, let's forget the young lady for a while and take your lovely wife home."

The Captain stood up, slipped the phone into his pocket, and climbed back up the stairs.

"There you are, love. Everything packed and ready to go?"

They climbed into the Mustang, and the Captain turned the key, and the V8 rumbled into life.

"Let's go home, love."

Chapter 40

BACK AT WORK

It was seven a.m. the next morning when the Captain walked into the squad room at the police station.

The chatter stopped immediately.

The Chief Detective spoke first. "Good morning, Captain."

"Good morning, all. Ready for another week?"

Heads nodded, but the squad room could see that the Captain was not quite one hundred percent, so it was better to say nothing than get singled out for a sharp question.

"Chief Detective, Sergeant, my office please."

They all went into the office and closed the door. Everyone else put their heads down and got to work.

"What has happened in my absence?"

The Chief Detective spoke first. "We have excavated the next victim, sir. That makes five now—four on the farm and one in the state forest."

"Did the chemist come up from head office to see if they could work out what was happening down in the cellar?"

"They arrived late yesterday, sir, as they were busy elsewhere, and they came directly here from their last job. They will be on it this morning."

"What is happening with the Federal police and the inquiry into the machine gun and RPG?"

"The army powers that be are stonewalling every request for information, sir."

"Keep pushing, and I will look into it through my sources as well."

"Sergeant, what about our friend, the sleazebag rapist?"

"He has been transferred to the remand centre at the main gaol. His defence lawyer went to the magistrate off the cuff to see if he could get bail, and he was told not to waste the accused's money, as he would be refused bail. So, he stays in remand until his case comes up. The victims have come forward and identified a lot of the clothing, and it has gone away for testing by the forensics lab in Sydney. They were happy that he was finally locked away."

"Right, thank you for the heads-up on everything. I will take a drive out to the farms later today. I just want to catch up with some paperwork first."

They both stood up, vacated the office, and closed the door.

The two officers looked at each other, both thinking the same thing. They expected the Captain to be on top of the world, but he was down in the dumps.

The Captain could not shake off the blues. He felt that his life was slipping away, and everywhere he turned, there was death and disappointment. The whole world was slowly sliding into moral decay and a lack of respect for each other.

The Captain slogged away at the paperwork for an hour, then decided that he had had enough. "Constable Wilkens."

"Yes, Captain. What can I do for you?"

"Get the keys for the van, and let's go and have a look at the progress at the farms."

"Right away, Captain. It's a lovely day for a drive in the country."

A few minutes later, they were pushing their way through the press people outside the police station.

"I was hoping these people would have all packed up and gone home when I got back, but they seem to have nothing better to do than hang around here, making a nuisance of themselves."

The constable never said anything, and they drove in silence to the farm.

"Which farm first, Captain?"

"Crack house first, and let's hope they can tell us something that we don't already know."

The constable wheeled the van into the crack farm and parked in the autumn sunshine.

They both exited the van and walked up to the entrance of the cellar.

The constable waited for the Captain to start down the steps while she looked about at the scene around the farmhouse. The Captain disappeared, and she followed him down the stairs and into the cellar.

There were a couple of chemists there examining the apparatus at various locations around the cellar.

The Captain spoke first. "Well, people, what conclusions have you come to?"

The head chemist looked up from what he was doing. "Well, Captain, I want to take some scrapings of various residue left in the beakers, but an educated guess is that they were manufacturing small quantities of explosives."

"What? Can you tell us what type of explosive?"

"Captain, with some chemical analysis, I can be more accurate, but I would say something like a plastic explosive, like the US Army C4 or Semtex."

"Is there any left here, or any raw material, or has it all been removed before the raid?"

"Nothing here now, Captain, just minor residue. I want to get this apparatus boxed and sent to the labs in Sydney for further investigation."

"This place is a real enigma with hidden cellars, drug labs, and heavy weapons. I wonder just how much they have manufactured and where the hell is it now. The commissioner will want to know about this ASAP. Right, get everything packed up and shipped back to Sydney as quickly as you can."

"Right, Constable, let's go over the road to where things are a little more orderly than this crack house."

The pair climbed into the van and headed across to the other farm.

"Explosives is the last thing we need around the country."

The van pushed its way through the press gathered at the entrance to the farm, and they ignored the shouted questions.

The pair exited into the autumn sunshine. They could see the backhoe working over in the trees, so they walked that way.

The head of forensics met them before they got to the backhoe.

"Yes, Captain, this is number four here on the farm, and as soon as we finish here with the backhoe, we will move over to the next suspect area."

The Captain muttered, "I think you will find another three graves before we are finished. However, these graves go back a long time— maybe forty or fifty years—and whether we will ever be able to identify the remains is another story. Have you exposed the remains yet?"

"Captain, we have found some human bones, so we are digging very carefully now, but you can say with certainty that it is a grave."

"OK. When you have exposed this grave, move on to the next one, but make sure that there are no more graves further away from the farmhouse."

"We are working out in small arcs around the farmhouse, Captain. If there is anyone buried there, then we will find their resting place."

With that, the Captain turned and started walking back to the van.

The constable's phone rang.

Unlisted number. "Good morning, Constable Wilkens here."

"Time Walker here. Just call me TW for short."

The constable was surprised. "What can I do for you, T.W.?"

"The Captain is depressed. Every time I ring, he feels it is all about death, and he has no control over it. On the weekend, I had him dig out the young lady who had been buried alive. Instead of being happy that they had saved her, it has depressed him. He needs to look at all the happiness he has brought into some people's lives and not the sadness that some people are feeling for their useless children. He is not looking at the big picture where he is bringing closure to people and saving people from the effects of drugs. I am a young person, so I cannot say the right things to the Captain. See what you can do, Constable. He has a lot of respect for you. Have a good day."

The phone went dead.

The constable walked a little faster and caught up to the Captain as he stood outside the van, looking at the press at the gate.

"Bloody ghouls."

"I will stop at the gate, Captain, while you ring the commissioner. I will give them the news about the latest find here on the farm, but we should keep the news about the explosives to ourselves at this time."

"Very good, Constable. Let's get it over with."

The Captain took out his phone but waited until they reached the gate before pushing the button for the Commissioner.

The constable walked up to the press with one of the uniformed branch officers with her.

"Good morning, people. Just a quick message this morning: we have found another burial place, which makes four sets of remains that we have found here. What I can say is that this set of remains is very old. It could be forty or fifty years old, going by the condition of the bones, so whether we can identify the remains or not will be determined by a forensic pathologist in Sydney.

We are searching for more remains and believe that we have found a couple of likely locations where the trees have grown over the graves. I will give you more information as we get it. Thank you."

"Constable, how many more do you expect to find?"

"We have a couple of likely locations; however, until we excavate, we cannot be sure of finding anything."

"Can we speak to the Captain?"

"No, the Captain is speaking to the police commissioner in Sydney at this moment, giving him a report on what is happening here."

"Good morning, all."

The constable turned and went back to the van, climbed in, and started the engine.

She made sure the windows were up, moved forward, and hit the siren and lights to move the press out of the way.

The Captain had reached the commissioner just as the constable got out to talk to the press.

"Good morning, Captain. What have you got for me today?"

"Well, Commissioner, we have unearthed grave number four on the farm; however, this one seems a lot older than the other ones to date. The forensic chemists have given me some disquieting news. It appears that they were manufacturing C4 or Semtex in the cellar under the crack house."

"What! Bloody hell, is there any explosive still there?"

"Only the stuff used on the booby trap on the door to the cellar. Other than that, nothing, sir. All we have is the apparatus they were using. They are packing it all up now to take back to Sydney for further tests.

I believe that a couple of the chemists that we have in gaol out here were responsible, and they were not making drugs. We will start to put some pressure on them now to find out just which ones are responsible."

"Keep me informed, Captain. Have a good day."

The van pulled away from the farm.

The Captain commented, "I'm not sure what has happened to the Commissioner, but he actually says goodbye now."

"Well, Captain, he is probably very happy that you have been able to expose so much criminal activity and bring it to a halt. This makes him look good as well. You and the Time Walker have done so much for so many people in such a short time. You deserve a pat on the back from the powers that be, however whether that will happen or not remains to be seen."

"Constable, I had not thought about it like that. We have all done very well working as a team. Now we need to start cleaning up the loose ends and start getting some convictions. I wish the forensic labs would get their fingers out so we have evidence to start prosecuting the likes of the rapist."

The Captain was silent for a moment as he looked about.

"The weather is beautiful in autumn, isn't it? The trees turning yellow, red, and brown, and the air crisp and clean with just a touch of winter. Stop at the coffee shop, Constable. My shout today."

"Thank you, Captain."

"They also make very good muffins as well. Let's get a couple of dozen for the people back in the squad room while we're there."

The constable found herself smiling, as it was good to see the Captain back to being his old self.

An hour later, they were back in the squad room, and everyone was enjoying a coffee and a muffin, courtesy of the Captain.

"Chief Detective, what do you think that mob was making plastic explosive for? What crimes use explosives? The only thing I can think of is terrorism. Anybody have any other thoughts on the matter, bring them to my or the Chief Detective's attention immediately."

The squad room was happy to see the Captain back to his old self.

Chapter 41

A TALK TO THE MAGISTRATE

It was early the next morning, and things were busy in the squad room.

"Chief detective, come into my office for a moment. Take a seat. Now, we have these chemists locked up, and we have been working on the principle that they were all making drugs. Now we find out that they were also making explosives, so we need to find out which ones were doing that and find out whatever we can about where they got the ingredients from, where the finished product went, and how much they made. Put our best people on interrogating them. Threaten them with long prison terms, and the drug chemists will probably dob them in."

"Changes the whole outlook on the buggers, doesn't it? I will get onto it straight away, Captain."

The Captain was sitting there, next moment by himself, musing on the way things were going when his phone rang.

"Good morning, young fellow. How are you on this beautiful Autumn day?"

"Very good, Captain. I see that the criminals were making plastic explosive in the crack farm?"

"Yes, my young friend. Now we have to find where it went to. Firstly, the only reason I can think you want plastic explosive for is terrorism, and I don't want fanatics running around with suicide vests using explosives manufactured in my neck of the woods."

"I understand, Captain, and I will look into it. However, it will be a long process as I don't know what time frame I need to start looking into."

"My friend, I have been doing some thinking into this matter, and I have been wondering whether the person who supplied the machine gun and the RPG could be involved. The chief of detectives has been working with the Federal police in Canberra trying to get information from the Army. However, they are being very obtuse about the whole matter. Maybe, just maybe, the army person is more than just a supplier of arms."

"OK, Captain, that is good thinking. I will use that as a starting point. It is a beautiful day, Captain. Maybe you need to go and have a talk to your magistrate friend and work out how we are going to convict these serial killers. Have a good day, Captain."

The phone went dead.

The Captain rang his mate, the chief magistrate.

"Hello, Captain. You have nearly sent me round the twist with your video. I have searched the whole reception area plus my chambers and cannot find any cameras. What's the real secret?"

"Well, that is what I am calling you about. Do you have an hour spare this morning?"

"For you, Captain. Yes. Come on up and have a coffee. Bring that laptop with you."

"Ok, we will be there in twenty minutes."

The phone line went dead.

"Constable Wilkens."

"Yes, Captain. You bellowed."

"Sorry for bellowing, but if they installed an intercom system here, a man would not need to bellow. Anyway, could you get the keys to the van and come with me to the courthouse?"

"No problem, Captain. Five minutes in the rear car park."

True to her word, they were in the van in five minutes. The Captain had his laptop with him.

"Coffee shop first, Constable, so we can get three muffins. The magistrate can supply the coffee. He has a magnificent coffee machine worthy of any coffee shop."

The constable pulled up outside the coffee shop.

"I will leave the van parked here. A visible police car slows down all the drivers."

The Captain got out.

"You mind the van, Captain. My shout today."

The constable was back in minutes. "Still hot, Captain, straight from the oven."

They parked in the courthouse car park and went up the steps into the reception area.

The magistrate opened the door to his chambers.

"Come on in, Captain, constable."

The Captain murmured to the constable. "I bet he has an intercom, that's how he knew we had arrived."

"Do I smell hot muffins, Constable?"

"Yes, sir. Captain said you liked hot muffins and that you would make us a hot coffee in exchange."

"Right, did he now? OK, what is your poison, constable?"

"A flat white for both myself and the Captain. One spoon of sugar each, please."

A few minutes later, they were seated in a small lounge area, sipping hot coffee and eating warm muffins.

"No lounge area like this in the police station, Captain."

"We would not even have a coffee machine if we had not chucked in fifty bucks each to buy one, and if we had not gotten a good discount from the Good Guys."

"Now, Captain, I have tried to work out how you had a video of myself last time you were here. Driving me nuts it is." The magistrate was scratching his head.

"Well, Andrew, that is why we are here. I will tell you a story, and the constable is the only other person who can vouch for the truth of it. Some time back, the constable was given a memory stick with a video on it, which showed an abduction of a young lady. I recognized some of the shop fronts, so we went and walked the street shown in the video. Same place, but twenty-five odd years ago. Checked out the van used in the abduction. Stolen and burnt out twenty-five years ago. Next, we got another memory stick that depicted two men burying something in the national park. When we investigated, we found our first victim buried there."

The magistrate went to speak, but the captain held up his hand. "Questions later."

"I started receiving phone calls from the young man who had walked into the police station and given the memory stick to the constable. He calls himself the Time Walker. He has developed a way to look back in time. He can't see the future, as that has not happened. The present is now, which everyone can see, but he can see the past.

Next, he gave us the location of the farm where we are finding the bodies and told me to get a search warrant before the guilty parties went out there and burnt the place down.

That was the first search warrant from yourself. Now, he has assisted us in all manner of inquiries. Without him, we would not be where we are today. He is a young person with a hatred of evil, and he was instrumental in giving myself and another fisherman the location of a young lady buried alive down the coast last weekend. Forget the dog digging story, that was for the press. We cannot disclose this young man, otherwise he will become a target for every criminal in the country who does not want to be exposed. Now, I am here today to show you some evidence to prove the above, but you must swear not to reveal any of this information to anyone. Call it client confidentiality. Do you agree to keep everything secret?"

"Captain, I find this all very strange, but you have my word that what we talk about today will never go outside these walls."

The Captain booted up his laptop and then handed it across to the magistrate.

The Time Walker had downloaded a lot of information about the crack house and the farm where the buried victims were being excavated.

He looked at the video of the rapist held in the cells and had to close his eyes when he saw the beating the girl was getting.

He handed the laptop back to the Captain. "I am happy that we have police officers like yourselves to get these criminals off the streets."

"Now, how can I help you, Captain?"

"I explained some of this before to you, but now we need some legal advice."

"Do you think that the videos could be introduced as evidence against people like the rapist in a court of law?"

"Captain, that is a moot point. How do you explain getting the video in the first place? A defence attorney would move to have these struck off as evidence, as he would not like any jury seeing what the defendant actually did. There is no precedent for anything like this. Never before have we been able to witness a crime that took place with no witnesses. The first such case would end up going all the way to the High Court if you did get a conviction."

"OK. We have enough evidence to convict the rapist with DNA and his assaults, and the same for the crack house people. We will have to look at how we can convict the killers of the young people buried out at the farm. Thank you for your opinion, and if you think of anything, please give me a call."

The Captain and Constable stood up, shook hands, and slowly left the courthouse.

The Captain's phone rang.

"Hello, young fellow. You saw the decision?"

"Yes, Captain. We will have to look at another way of getting a conviction. I have a few ideas, and I want these people to be punished for what they have done. By the way, Captain, I am making progress on the supplier of the weapons to the crack house. There is quite a little business going on there, and yes, they do have the explosives, but more on that later. Have a good day, the pair of you."

The Captain looked at the Constable and shook his head.

"He is always on the go, isn't he? I would like to meet him one day in person."

"Me too, Captain. He certainly is different from the normal run-of-the-mill young people."

They were soon back at the police station.

The Captain rang the police commissioner in Sydney.

The phone was answered, once again almost immediately. "Good morning, Captain. How might I assist?"

"Just touching base with you, Commissioner, to let you know that we believe the supplier of the weapons is also the recipient of the explosives. When we know more, we will be working out a plan to get all of it into police custody."

"I really hope that your information is correct, Captain. The very thought of that being out there in the marketplace has given me sleepless nights since you reported what they were making at that crack house. Now, some good news: We should have some DNA evidence back to you later today on the first victim you found in the state park."

They ended the call, with the commissioner wishing the captain a good day.

The Captain could still not get over the change in the commissioner.

"Chief detective, a moment please?"

"Yes, Captain."

"What's the status of the interrogation of the chemists now that we know they were also making explosives?"

"Captain, we have our best two interrogators working these chemists up at the remand centre. They have been threatened with withholding evidence and that they will get longer sentences unless they let us know everything that was being manufactured in the cellar, how much was manufactured, and where it went to. Our people should be back very soon with some answers."

"How are you getting on with your Federal police mate in Canberra and the source of the weapons to the crims?"

"Well, the army major we are dealing with in the supply chain is resisting very strongly about giving up any information. The Federal police are now working with the Army police to try and get an investigation going into missing weapons. However, the same people we suspect of selling the weapons are the same people who will investigate any shortage on the inventory at the armoury. Very incestuous arrangements these armed forces have when it comes to dealing with them."

"Keep pushing them every day, because I suspect any plastic explosives also ended up with the same people."

The Captain let his thoughts wander across everything that had happened over the last couple of weeks. So many different types of crimes, and how were they going to get convictions against all the people they had arrested? The crimes that depended on physical evidence, such as fingerprints and DNA and witness identification, seemed so simple compared to the serial killers of crimes committed long ago with no eyewitness and no physical evidence directly connected to the killers. He wondered what the Time Walker was thinking. As far as he was concerned, his evidence of being able to see the event should be enough to send the criminals away to gaol for their crimes was simplistic considering the way the law had become so confusing to the layperson.

Well, time would tell.

The sun went down earlier as the days got shorter, with winter just around the corner.

The Captain called it a day, wondering what tomorrow would bring.

The day dawned into what the Yanks called an Indian Summer day. Beautiful sunshine and a crisp, clean sky, and fresh winds. The precursor to winter with its overcast days, frosts, and light rains for days on end. Well, thought the Captain, we must take what God gives us and be thankful.

He had breakfast with his wife and then walked through the back laneways to the rear of the police station, arriving at seven-thirty AM. The squad room was already full, with the night and day shifts overlapping, and all the detectives already there enjoying a coffee and a quick catch-up with their colleagues.

"Good morning, all. Are we ready for another busy day?"

A nodding of heads and a few "yes sir" greeted the Captain.

The Captain made a cup of tea and he headed towards his office.

He had just sat down when his phone rang.

A quick glance at the unlisted number, and then, "Good morning, young fellow. How are you this morning?"

"Very well, thank you, Captain. Now, an update on the army. I was fortunate last night to catch the army major just as he left his office. I am getting better at following cars now, what with my new equipment, and I followed him for 30 minutes as he drove out of Canberra and up into the hills where he has a property. Very isolated, with the last 5 kilometres being a dirt road. He has quite a setup there behind barbed wire security fences. Rifle ranges and grenade ranges and obstacle courses. I thought I was looking at the regular army, even down to the recruits running around the place. Everyone was wearing camo gear with a distinguishing strip so they could all recognize each other. I then realized that I was looking at a homegrown militia, just like they have in the good old US of A. I am not sure at this time, but assume that all the weapons are being supplied by the regular Australian Army, even though they don't know it at this time. The drug manufacturing could have been financing all of this setup, but I still need to find where the explosives have gone to. Have a good day, Captain."

The Captain sat there stunned. This was nothing like he was expecting. A homegrown militia. Visions of the Oklahoma bombing came to mind. Bloody hell, he needed to speak to the commissioner.

As usual, the commissioner answered the phone before it had rung twice.

"Good morning, Captain. What have you got for me?"

"Not good news, Commissioner. The young fellow tells me that the army major who we suspect of selling the weapons is actually building up his own homegrown militia, right down to the training camp, rifle ranges, etc. Just over the border from the ACT in NSW. What do we do if this turns out to be correct? Do we go it alone, talk to ASIO, get the Federal police involved? SAS? Remember, the more people involved, the greater the risk of a leak to the Army Major or the press."

Stony silence from the other end of the phone.

"Are you there, Commissioner?"

"Yes, Captain. That's a curly one you have sprung on me. Let's keep it to ourselves for the moment. Let's wait until we can verify everything. In the meantime, I will see what I can find regarding protocols for something like this. Please keep me up to date as you get more information. Good day, Captain."

Chapter 42

A HOME-GROWN MILITIA

The Captain went back to thinking about the whole scenario. Why would the Army Major want explosives? Because they do not keep explosives in magazines along with rifles and machine guns. They would be kept at locations that he does not control. He does not have access to explosives. What would he want explosives for? Is he going to blow up a building? He would need a lot of Semtex to destroy a building, but not if he has access to ANFO, which is made from Ammonium Nitrate and Fuel Oil in the right ratio. Ammonium Nitrate would be a lot easier to access.

The Semtex would be a good booster to set off the ANFO. What targets would he want to blow up? Parliament House sprung to mind. He is based in Canberra. Bloody hell, with a militia to step in after Parliament was blown up, it could make the Major the first President of Australia. It sounded far-fetched, but in the mind of a schizophrenic, nothing is too far-fetched.

A lot of young people are disillusioned with democracy, and they don't know their history of socialist countries like Russia, Nazi Germany, and Cuba.

He needed more information.

The whole list of options made his head reel.

He would just have to wait for the Commissioner and the Time Walker to get back to him.

The Captain slowly waded through the paperwork that had built up on his desk, and it was nearing lunchtime when he got another phone call from his young friend.

"Hello, young fellow. How has your day been?"

"Well, Captain, I am confused about what they are doing with the explosives. They have four tip trucks that are full of powder, and they have hidden some of the Semtex in every truck.

The trucks are all painted the same colour and look to have a builder's name on the doors.

They have a workshop that is cutting up steel pipe and welding brackets onto the pipes, then they have welded flat pieces top and bottom onto the pipes. A man with a cutting torch is cutting a piece out of the side of the pipe. They have people filling the pipes with Semtex, and it looks like nails. Then a man clamps a piece of plastic pipe on the outside of the pipe to cover the slot that they cut into the steel pipe.

Lastly, they bolt the pipes onto the outside of the Land Cruiser utilities that they have. The Land Cruisers all look like army vehicles.

I have never seen anything like this on 4-wheel drives before."

The Captain was horrified.

"Are you listening, Captain?"

"Yes. What you are describing, young fellow, is 4 truck bombs filled with 'ANFO' (Ammonium Nitrate Fuel Oil explosive).

The Semtex will be the booster to set the bombs off.

The pipes that you are describing are homemade Claymore mines. Clamped onto the outside of the Land Cruiser, they can be detonated, and the blast blows all the nails outwards, away from the Land Cruiser, killing anybody within 100 meters.

This is horrific, and it looks like they will be using them very soon if they have the truck bombs ready. There are new detonators available now that can be activated wirelessly, so nobody needs to be anywhere near them when they blow up.

We need to do something about them very quickly, as I believe they could be going to try and blow up the Houses of Parliament, and the Major could be going to try and use his militia to make him President.

Sounds crazy, but crazy things have happened before.

Can you send me a video of the trucks, if possible? I need to get the Commissioner and the tactical response on this right away."

"Captain, you will have a video within the hour. Goodbye."

The phone went dead.

The Captain called the Commissioner, and the phone was answered almost immediately.

"Captain. What news?"

"Not good, Commissioner. Looks like they have four truck bombs with the Semtex as the boosters to set the ANFO off. Plus, they are using Semtex to make Claymore mines, which are being bolted onto Land Cruisers painted to resemble army vehicles. They are not far from being ready, and I think Parliament House is the target. I also think our Army Major thinks he could then take over as leader of the country with his militia. I think we have a raving nutter on our hands."

The Commissioner was silent.

"Are you there, Commissioner?"

"Yes, Captain. I was trying to convince myself that I did not hear what you just told me was true."

"Commissioner, my mate has promised a video in an hour or so because he could not work out what was happening until I explained it all to him. He has never seen anything like this before."

"Captain, I am going to get the tactical response Captain here in my office. You still have a chopper and a few tactical response people with you out there. Get yourself and your laptop and whatever tech people you can into the chopper and get down here to Sydney as soon as possible. I don't think we have time to find out what procedure we should follow. I will also find out from the chemist if they were making Semtex, just to ensure we are not chasing fairies at the bottom of the garden. I will be looking out for you. Goodbye."

The Captain bellowed, "Constable, Chief of Detectives."

They both appeared at the door to see the Captain putting his bulletproof vest on and his shoulder holster and pistol on.

"Yes, sir," they both answered.

"Constable, chase up the head of the tactical response team and any officers that are still here, and get the chopper pilots ready for a flight to Sydney. I will be going with them. Chief Detective, you are in charge until I come back. I am not sure how long I will be away, and I am sorry I am not at liberty to give you any more information."

The two officers turned and disappeared, calling on the radios and making phone calls.

Five minutes later, the officers that were in the police station, along with the chopper pilots, were headed to the helipad.

Within fifteen minutes, the chopper lifted off and headed toward police headquarters for the state in Sydney.

It was a quick trip, and the chopper landed on the helipad at police headquarters.

The head of tactical response was waiting at the chopper pad.

"Follow me, Captain."

It was a quick walk through a maze of offices and lecture rooms and then upstairs to the police Commissioner's office.

They rapped on the door, and a voice called to come in. The Commissioner stood up, came around the desk, and shook the Captain's hand. "Please sit down. I have ordered a pot of coffee and some biscuits. This information that you have given me is very disquieting, Captain. I do hope that for once your information is incorrect."

At that moment, the Captain's phone rang.

"Time Walker here. Boot up your computer, Captain. There is a long video on there that you all need to watch. If you need to speak to me, Captain, hold your phone above your head, and I will call within a few minutes. You need to get a remote earplug so I can speak to you at any time. Talk soon."

The Captain had his computer out and was waiting for it to boot up.

On the front page was a large file marked "Militia." The Captain clicked on it, and they waited for it to boot up. The Commissioner pressed his intercom button and told his secretary to get an IT person to his office immediately.

"We will plug your computer into this large screen here so we all get a better view."

The IT person arrived with a cable. "Knew what you wanted, Commissioner."

A minute later, the file came up on the large screen.

The three officers pulled up chairs and waited while the video started.

The first view was of the road coming into the farm and a 2.4-meter-high fence with barbed wire on top. A pair of gates were closed with the name of Cool Mountain Deer Farm on a sign. The video went along the road for a few kilometres, and then a cluster of buildings appeared. A main administration building and some buildings that appeared to be farm workshops and low buildings that the assumption was barracks.

The view changed into the workshop, and the four dump trucks were sitting there with the name of a building renovation company. The officers could see the subtle changes to the trucks: steel plate welded to the tops of the bodies and steel slats welded to cover the radiator, but still allowing air to pass under and up through the slats, then through the radiators.

The area around the driver's position was also plated to stop small arms fire.

The view then moved across to where they were fixing the claymore mines onto the Land Cruisers—two rows of eight down each side.

There was also armour for the driver and down both sides to protect anyone sitting in the rear of the utilities.

The view changed as a person walked out the door into the area of the parking lot, where there were a number of buses all painted to resemble army vehicles. The next scenes were of machine gun pits ringing the whole area of the buildings. The officers counted ten positions, all sited to provide covering fire for each gun pit.

The last scene was of a lecture hall with large maps on the front wall. A group of Militia were studying the maps and making corrections. One large map was easily identifiable as Parliament House; the other looked like a big shopping mall.

The video came to an end.

The three officers sat silently, looking at a blank screen and wondering just what they were going to do.

The Commissioner spoke first.

"Well, gentlemen, what do we do?"

Captain Wilson spoke first.

"Well, they are very well organized along the lines of an army unit. I would not be surprised if the trucks do not have foam-filled tires so that they cannot be punctured by bullets or spikes. We do have one advantage, and that is they are boxed into a valley with one way in and the same way out. It has allowed them the privacy to build everything that they have there and train their people, but they have to get them out to undertake their mission, whatever it might be."

The Tactical Response Captain spoke next. "Captain Wilson is correct. There are a number of creeks coming down from the hills, and the road crosses them across some quite decent culverts. If we waited until this evening when the whole complement of Militia are in the compound and blew up two or three of those larger culverts, then we would have them trapped in their own camp."

"Both good observations, Captains. Now, do we have the explosives to do that?"

The Tactical Response Captain spoke. "No, we don't, Commissioner. However, not far from the Deer Farm front gate, there is a large quarry that supplies a lot of rock to the Canberra construction industry. We can requisition what we want from there. We have, as part of our outfit, quite a few ex-army demolition experts who will take out two or three bridges or culverts so no truck or four-wheel drive will be able to get out along that road."

"We should not blow the road unless they make a break for it, as we might need to get vehicles along the road. Last resort. All agree?"

A nodding of heads.

The Commissioner replied. "How about you two guys getting together and working out a plan? If possible, I would like to shut them down tonight, as we cannot run the risk of them driving out of the farm later tonight. Take as many men as you need and all the choppers, and get down there to Canberra as quickly as you can. I will contact the Chief of Police for the New South Wales area that surrounds The Australian Capital Territory and bring him up to speed so he can provide some Traffic Branch people for evacuations of any farms in the area and sealing the whole area off from the public. He will also arrange for your men to pick up what explosives they need to take out the access road if necessary. Captain, pick up an earpiece for your phone from my secretary on the way out. Please keep in touch, but

Captain Wilson, this is your operation. You have the final call on anything, and I will convey that to the Captain down there near Canberra. On your way, gentlemen, and please don't take any risks."

The two field Captains stood up and left the Commissioner's office.

The Captain picked up his earpiece and said to the Tactical Response Captain, "I don't know how I ended up being in charge and being held responsible."

"You will be right, mate, but why do you need an earpiece for your phone?"

"I have an undercover person feeding me information, and he needs to be able to contact me at a moment's notice."

"Rather him than me, mate. Now, tell me, while we are flying down there, how we are going to neutralize this mob. I have all my people, not flying with us, already on the road in our armoured vehicles. They will drive all the way with flashing lights until they get to within 20 kilometres of the place. Once we call on them to surrender, the proverbial will hit the fan."

"From what we saw, they have armoured all the trucks and the Land Cruisers, and they have a few buses to carry their troops into Canberra. We are going to end up with a bigger bun fight than the Waco Davidians fiasco, and we don't have any tanks."

"You are just a bundle of cheer, mate. I know that they will dig in, and whoever has to dig them out will pay dearly. How did this ever happen, and why did the Army not pick up on this guy stealing weapons? What has ASIO been doing all this time?"

The chopper, accompanied by other choppers, pushed the limits on the time to get to Canberra. Before they knew it, they were swooping in to land at the police academy.

There was a senior officer in uniform waiting for them as they got out and walked away from the chopper.

He introduced himself and asked, "Could somebody bring me up to speed with what is happening? I have had the commissioner order me to get some explosives for you Tactical Response people and that I am to provide whatever assistance I am asked for. Has World War Three started?"

The Captain shook his head. "I am beginning to think so, Captain. Let's get into your squad car and head out to this address, and we will bring you up to date as we drive."

They stopped short of the entrance by some five kilometres and parked in a truck rest area.

By this time, the Canberra Captain was shaking his head. "How the hell are we going to get them to give themselves up? They are better armed than we are by the sound of things."

"Captain, all we can do at the moment is confine them in their valley and not let them loose with their trucks and Land Cruisers. We do not want to expose any of our people to those claymore mines, as they are full of nails and very deadly."

The car park was filling up with police vehicles. One of the tactical response personnel came across and let them know that they had gotten hold of some cases of gelignite, detonators, and Cordex.

The Captain's phone rang in his ear.

"Yes, young fellow?"

"Captain, the Major has just turned into the access road to the farm, and he has the sergeant from the armoury with him. There is a lot of activity at the Deer Farm. I don't like what is happening, Captain."

"Right, stay in touch. We are going to mine a couple of the bridges on the way into the farm so they cannot escape."

"You need to hurry, Captain."

"We are on our way."

"Right, let's get those bridges mined as quickly as possible. The Major and his sergeant have gone into the farm."

The tactical response vehicles, which were arriving, followed the police vehicle along the road to the turnoff to the Deer Farm. They had not gone very far when they came to a small creek with steep banks and flowing water.

"Right, this one will do. Get the demolition guys working on this one," ordered the Captain.

Tactical officers spilled out of the armoured vehicles and were down the bank, digging holes under the roadway. The Captain drove on another few hundred meters and came to another creek, very similar, with steep banks and a small trickle of water running through the culvert. "This one will do as well. Captain, get some of your men working on this one as well."

The Captain's phone rang again in his ear.

"Captain, the Major and the sergeant are rallying all the troops into the buses, and they are getting the drivers into the trucks and Land Cruisers. The trucks are revving their engines. I can see exhaust smoke, and there is a lot of activity with soldiers loading weapons into the buses and Land Cruisers."

"They will be onto us before we can blow up any of the bridges, and with those claymore mines, it will be a massacre," lamented the Captain.

"Captain, I don't think these people will surrender. They are the same as what were at the crack farm and will fight it out."

"I am afraid you are right, young fellow."

Night was falling as the police officers did the best they could to dig in around the two small bridges, but the Captain knew it would not be enough, and they would not be able to blow the bridges in time to stop the small army.

Chapter 43

AN EARLY BLAST

The flash of light lit up the whole sky over where the Renegade army camp was. It filled the valley from side to side in one stupendous ball of flame.

"Everyone down on the ground! I think the explosive trucks have gone up; there will be a shock wave."

Everyone threw themselves onto the ground as a blast of air ripped down the valley, uprooting trees and ripping limbs off the bigger trees. Then there was the sound of a thousand thunderclaps all at once, which was deafening. Police clamped their hands over their ears. Nobody had ever heard anything like this before. Next, there was a wind going back towards the camp as the flame consumed all the oxygen over the camp, and a massive mushroom cloud rose in the air, boiling with flame to illuminate everything in the valley. People lay about moaning in pain as eardrums had been burst. There were secondary explosions going off, but they were diminishing as the flame slowly died out after consuming all its fuel.

Slowly, people started climbing to their feet.

Nobody could understand what anybody was saying, but a police vehicle drove up from down the road. The driver found the captain and took a notebook out of his pocket and wrote, Ambulances are on their way. What happened?

The Captain spoke. "I think there was an explosion that set all the 4 trucks off in a big blast. Get an armoured vehicle up here so I can go and have a look and see if there are any survivors. Get the paramedics to check out our people for injuries, and I don't think we need to worry about mining the small bridges."

The officer nodded and spoke into his radio.

Within minutes, the Captain of the Tactical Response arrived and signalled the Captain to come with him in the armoured vehicle. The Captain put his hand up to his ear and felt blood running down the side of his neck. The flashing lights of ambulances arriving were comforting to the Captain.

He climbed into the armoured vehicle with the Captain, and they drove slowly up the valley with their lights on high beam and a rotating spotlight, which picked up shattered trees everywhere. The gate to the farm was gone.

When they arrived at where the camp was, the only recognisable things were the foundations of the buildings and parts of trucks, such as an engine block or rear diff with the odd wheel attached.

Everything and every person were gone, as if they had never been there in the first place. A giant broom of fire had swept the whole place away. The two captains climbed out and looked around in awe at the power of fifty cubic metres of ANFO exploding in one massive blast.

They both stood there, shaking their heads.

The Captain tapped the Tactical Response Captain on the shoulder and indicated they should leave the place. He mouthed tomorrow, and the Tactical Captain nodded his head in agreement. They turned the armoured vehicle around and headed down the road. When they met up with the rest of the squads, the Captain wrote a note and handed it to the senior officer.

"No one to enter until I have had a look at the place in daylight tomorrow morning."

The officer spoke to a constable, and they got some police tape out and strung it across the road. The two captains went looking for the Captain from Canberra.

He was back organising the removal of the explosives from the bridges and getting a roll call done.

Captain Peters showed him the note about no entry until the Captain was there in daylight.

He got a nod in reply and a written note.

See the ambulance as both of you are bleeding from the ears, and then go to the academy. You will find a meal and a place to sleep. I will ensure that everything is looked after here.

Both Captains gave a nod of thanks and headed down to the ambulances.

The paramedics checked them out. "Busted eardrums, guys, but you were very lucky."

The captain handed him his notebook.

The paramedic wrote.

"Sorry mate. Busted eardrums. You need to see a specialist tomorrow. Quite a few tonight, along with a few splinters of timber and the odd broken arm, but no one killed. What happened?"

The Captain nodded his head. Suddenly he felt very tired. A police constable came over and indicated to the pair to follow him. Within minutes, they were heading down the dirt road and back towards the academy, a hot shower, something to eat, and some blessed sleep.

It was a hot shower with the water as hot as he could stand, then a burst of cold water to cool him down. He realised that he had no other clothes, but on the bed was a bathrobe. His clothes were gone, but his bulletproof vest, handgun, and harness were folded neatly on the bed. One thing about staying in a police academy...

There was a knock on the door, and a young constable indicated to follow him to the dining room. He padded along in his bare feet and was joined by the Tactical Response Captain.

The next moment, a plate with a big T-bone, chips and vegetables, and gravy was placed in front of them. Both of them were handed a small bottle of pills, and the constable indicated it was for their earaches.

The pair devoured the steaks, chips, and veggies, then stood up. The constable was there to escort them both back to their rooms.

The door closed on the Captain as he lay back on the bed, which was the last thing he remembered before he dropped off to sleep.

Habit woke the Captain at 5am, like it always did.

His clothes had been washed and ironed and were neatly laid out beside the bed on a small table. His shoes had been shined, and there was a small bottle of water beside the bottle of pills. He read the directions on the bottle and took two pills. A quick hot shower and he was dressed and ready by 5:30am.

He opened the bedroom door, and a different constable was there to escort him to the dining room. Bacon and eggs, a hash brown, and toast with a mug of coffee were soon being eaten. The Tactical Response Captain was there, finishing his breakfast as well.

Then it was back to the bedroom to dress with the bulletproof vest, the shoulder holster, and the Glock, all covered by the coat.

He felt his pocket, and there was his phone. He sent his wife an SMS that he was in Canberra and would be home as soon as possible. The phone chirped, and it was the Time Walker. Good to see you up and about, Captain. I will talk later when your ears are better.

The Tactical Response Captain and Captain Wilson walked outside, and there waiting for them was a squad car. The doors were opened, and the pair piled into the back seat.

35 minutes later, they stopped at the police tape across the road.

Also waiting were some of the forensic people that the Captain was getting to know so well.

"All right, people, my apologies, I am not hearing well, but let's go up to what's left of the camp and see if we can get an understanding of what happened."

Once again, they all piled into vehicles and drove up but stopped short of the camp proper.

They all climbed out and walked up to what was once the car park area.

The asphalt was gone from the ground. The building was totally gone except for a few sections of concrete foundations. Everywhere they looked was total devastation. There were no bodies as they had been consumed as fuel in the fireball that lit up the whole valley. There were no weapons other than twisted pieces of steel embedded into the ground. Trees had been uprooted and burned as fuel. Further up the valley sides, the trees had been stripped of all their branches, and not a tree for two hundred metres had any leaves.

"My God, I have never seen anything like this. It is like the photos you see in books of Hiroshima."

"Thanks, be that they never got to explode these bombs in a shopping mall or on the freeway at peak hour."

"I am not sure what you forensic people are going to do here, but make sure that you get plenty of photos of the devastation. I am suddenly wanting to go back to my little country town."

He took his phone out of his pocket and saw that it had been fully charged and pressed the number for the commissioner.

The phone was answered instantly.

"Captain."

"Sorry sir, I am not hearing very well as I have busted eardrums, but I am certain that we don't need to worry about the explosives that were manufactured. The Semtex, along with fifty cubic metres of ANFO, all went up last evening in one gigantic blast that took out everything in the militia camp. Forensics will get photos; however, if you think of Hiroshima, you are pretty well on the money.

I will head back home today and leave forensics to try and make some sense out of all this, but there is not much here to give anybody any understanding of what happened. I do know if they had got this stuff out into the streets of Canberra, it would have been mass murder on a grand scale."

The Captain heard the commissioner say, "Thank you for everything that you have done, and thank the young fellow when next you are talking to him."

The Captain turned to the Tactical Response Captain. "Any chance of a lift home, mate?"

He got a nod, and the pair turned and walked away, leaving it to forensics to make some sense of it all.

40 minutes later, the pair were on a chopper heading for the Captain's hometown. The countryside looked beautiful in the greens, golds, reds, and browns of autumn.

The chopper came in over the police station and landed. The rotor was still turning. The two Captains shook hands, and Captain Wilson climbed out, ducked his head, and walked away as the chopper revved up. He turned and gave a wave and walked towards the police van that had arrived.

"Good morning, Constable Wilkins. How have things been in my absence?"

"Captain, you have only been away for one day."

"The description on the news did not tell us much. What do you want to do first?"

"Go to the hospital as I have burst eardrums, and I am not hearing very well."

"On our way, Captain."

Two hours later, after having his ears cleaned and seeing the specialist, he was hearing a lot better. The Constable was waiting for him, and they headed back towards the police station. The newspaper ghouls were noticeably thinner on the ground as they had all headed off to Canberra and the mysterious explosion that had occurred on the deer farm.

The Constable spoke, "Well, Captain, what was the story of the blast and the busted eardrums?"

"Coffee and a muffin, Constable, is the cost of finding out, but my house first so I can say hello to the wife."

They pulled up outside the Captain's house, and within seconds, his wife was there at the front gate.

"Are you all right, Robert? Have you been down to Canberra yesterday?"

"Yes, love, in an advisory capacity only. I seem to have picked up some sort of ear infection, so I went to the doctor first thing, and he said all will be good in a few days. I do have to get back to the station, but how about we go for a pizza and a bottle of red wine this evening?"

"That would be nice, Robert. I will be ready to go by six p.m. Have a good day, love."

The Captain got in the van, and they headed for the coffee shop.

"Well, Constable, I realized yesterday that the person selling the weapons and the ones making the explosives could be one and the same people. So, our mate the Time Walker investigated and found out that the Army major had built up his own militia on a farm up in the hills outside Canberra. Further investigation revealed 4 truckloads of ANFO, and the Semtex was being used to make Claymore mines, which were being attached to the front and side of all the vehicles.

The Commissioner wanted me in Sydney immediately, and we had a quick meeting with Tactical Response, and then I find myself on a chopper heading to Canberra with a convoy of Armoured vehicles and in charge of the whole shebang.

Very long story, but the Army major had visions of leading Australia by blowing up Parliament House and taking over. A raving nutter, but so was Adolf Hitler, and look what harm he caused.

Well, to cut a long story short, they were leaving to go and attack their targets when the four truckloads of ANFO, about 50 cubic metres in all, went up at once just as they were about to leave their base camp. The blast was unbelievable. We were about 3 kilometres from the camp, and we got injuries like busted eardrums and broken arms.

I have never seen or heard anything like it. Hiroshima is the closest I can use to describe the destruction. Not one survivor and nothing left of their camp."

"Here is the coffee shop."

"My shout, Captain."

The Constable headed for the counter.

The Captain rang his counterpart in Canberra.

"Good morning, Captain Rob. How are you today?"

"Mate, sorry to have left everything for you to clean up. I was really a bit shell-shocked over the whole incident."

"Not a worry, but I found out an interesting bit of information when I took the unused explosives back to the quarry. They had a break-in about 5 days ago, and they had 4 sets of Orica WEBGEN wireless blasting systems, which are a new wireless type detonator. All programmable and able to transmit a signal through rock and concrete. Very sophisticated but foolproof, so I am surmising that the militia were the thieves, and the only person who knew the code to fire them would be the Major, so he decided to go out in a blaze of glory, so to speak, and detonated the whole lot."

"Do you think that these things could be hacked?"

"No way, Robert. The password is 10 to the 10th, which is 100 billion different combinations of numbers. You would need to be an electronic genius to be able to crack that code. Anyway, none of our people were killed, and the threat is gone, but we need to be aware of these types of people.

Nice meeting you, and no worries regarding the clean-up, but you owe me a beer for cleaning up your mess. Bye, mate."

The Constable arrived back with the coffee and a muffin, and life was good, but the Captain's thoughts were on electronic genius and code-breaking, or a Time Walker looking on as the Major programmed the detonators. Sending the code to fire them would not be hard for him.

"Deep in thought, Captain?"

"Just thinking of the death and destruction that could have eventuated if not for the young fellow getting that information to me."

"Good coffee, Constable, and the muffins are great." The Captain called the waiter over and asked for a couple of dozen muffins to takeaway. "Must remember the boys and ladies back at the station."

The office had not changed in his absence, and the people were happy to hoe into a muffin. The coffee machine was getting a real workout, and everyone was curious about what they saw on the news.

"Well, people, I got to work with some great officers in the last day or so. The blast was self-detonated by a raving nutter, who had visions of ruling Australia. Keep watching the news for more information."

With that, he headed to the office and some solitude.

He closed the door and rang the Commissioner.

"Good afternoon, Captain. How are your ears recovering?"

"Well, Sir, they have had a lot of dry blood washed out, and they are starting to heal."

"What sort of feedback have we got from the Federal Police and Army, sir?"

"Nothing, Captain. They don't want to be associated with the explosion, and ASIO is embarrassed that a militia had been operating so close to Canberra, and they did not know."

I spoke to the Captain down Canberra way, and he mentioned the theft of the new Orica blasting system, and he thinks that it was the militia that stole them. So, whatever we do find out down the road, it is best to let sleeping dogs lie. You and the young fellow saved hundreds, if not thousands, of lives."

"I understand, Commissioner."

"Once again, Captain, my thanks, and my thanks to the young fellow."

The phone went dead.

The Captain was musing on the whole operation when his phone rang.

"Hello, young fellow. Tell me now, did you know the sequence of numbers for the detonators?"

"Evil people, Captain, as evident by their intent to kill a lot of innocent people.

Have a nice evening with your wife, and the seafood pizza is very good. Talk soon."

The young fellow did not seem in any way affected by the death of all the militia, but like he said, they were evil people intent on killing innocent people.

The Captain closed his office and headed for home and a nice evening out with his wife.

The next morning, the Captain received the DNA results for the first remains excavated in the national forest.

It matched one of the families that had lost a daughter 20 years before.

The Captain rang his mate, the magistrate.

"Hello, Captain. Were you anywhere near that bomb blast two nights ago down near Canberra?"

"Mate, you will need to speak a bit slower and a bit louder as I am recovering from ruptured eardrums. I nearly drove the wife insane last night in the restaurant asking her to repeat herself."

"Say no more, Captain, you have just answered my question. That will be another beer when we finally get together. Now, what can I do for you?"

"Mate, we have identified the first set of remains from the National Forest. The bones will be returned to the family in the next couple of days. Should they hold off burying them until we convict the guilty parties?"

"Captain, that would be cruel, however, do not let them cremate the bones. If we go to court and the defence contests the results of the DNA, we can always exhume them, though that is hard on the families also. Do you have any suspects yet?"

"Not at this time, and I am not sure how we will get any evidence to convict anyone."

"What about your friend the Time Walker? Can he help?"

"Well, he can probably tell me who they are, but how do I get evidence to convict them without reasonable doubt?"

"I see your problem. Anything else I can help you with?"

"No, mate, thanks for your time." The Captain hung up.

Chapter 44

FIRST DNA RESULTS

"Chief Detective."

"Yes, sir."

"Have we got any information back from the Lands Department yet on who has owned the land?"

The detective held up an envelope. "Just this minute opened the mail, and here is the information on the land ownership going back one hundred years to when it was first broken away from the large holding in the area. It has always been held by the one family since about 1920. Passed down from father to son all that time. The current owner is in a retirement village. His wife passed away some years back. He is suffering from dementia, and his two twin sons, both in their sixties, are fighting over ownership. They used to be very close until the father got dementia, and who would have power of attorney has caused a split between them. We cannot find any evidence of the place ever being leased out either."

"Well, Captain, that sort of narrows the suspects down a bit. Now, how do we get any evidence on who is the guilty party?"

"Leave it with me, Chief Detective, and would you be so good as to send Constable Wilkens in? Please."

A knock on the door a couple of minutes later saw the Constable enter.

"Please sit down, Constable. Well, we now know whose remains we have exhumed from the national forest. Please read the DNA report, and there is the report done by the forensic people. I don't want the family or anyone else to see the report on the horrific injuries that this girl suffered. You have already met this family when you got DNA swabs from them?"

"That's correct, Captain."

"Constable, I would like them to be notified that their daughter's remains will be returned to them in a few days' time. I want the remains to go direct to an undertaker. Now, should you and I go and see the family?"

"Captain, I think that would be a nice gesture of respect."

"OK. Could you call them and ask if they are at home? If they are, we go immediately. Not a duty that I like, but one that has to be done along with a lot of other not-nice duties."

"I will do that immediately, Captain."

The Constable left the office.

The Captain's phone rang.

"Hello, young fellow. How can I help you today?"

"Captain, your people are almost done excavating on the farm. When they have completed their duties there, I will send you a horrific video of the evil people who did these crimes so they can face their punishment for their evil deeds."

"Time Walker, how do I get evidence to convict them?"

"Already underway, Captain. Now the Constable is coming for you. Good day, Sir."

A knock at the Captain's door.

"Coming, Constable."

"The van is ready, Captain."

"Well, let's get it over with, Constable."

They drove out of the backyard of the police station through the last remaining press people.

"Looks like the rest have rushed off to the bombing down in Canberra," remarked the Captain.

"Captain, when the bomb story hit the television news, there was a scramble of people into vehicles outside the police station, and the street was almost empty."

"Well, a fresh sheep died elsewhere, so the vultures were off for a new meal elsewhere."

Silence settled on the pair of them as they drove across town. Both of them were lost in thoughts of the family they were going to meet.

A few minutes later, the Constable parked the car in front of a neat, low-set house.

"This is the family's house, Captain. Another well-kept house and yard holding so much grief. Come on, Captain, before I start to cry."

They both exited the faithful van and walked up to the front door, which opened just as they arrived.

"Please come in, officers. The wife has just put the kettle on. Would you like tea or coffee?" The words were spoken by a gentleman with grey hair.

The Constable spoke for the two of them.

"Coffee, please. White with two sugars."

"Please take a seat. My wife will be here in a minute."

The gentleman picked up a colour photograph of a young woman with blonde hair.

"This is the last photo taken of our daughter, just two days before she disappeared. All these years, we have lived in hope that she would open the front door and walk inside."

A tear trickled down his weathered cheeks, which he mopped at with a handkerchief.

"My apologies, officers. Here is the wife with the coffee and biscuits."

The Captain spoke first.

"We have received the results of the DNA tests that were done on the body removed from the national park, and the DNA from the body matches the DNA from yourself and your wife without any possibility of error. We are very sorry to be the bearer of this news and to be the ones who have taken away any hope of your daughter being alive."

The wife spoke the first words since the officers had entered the house.

"I know you, Captain. I have seen you grow up, and we understand. However, as parents, we have always had our hopes. Now we can give our daughter a decent burial, and we can finally move on. We have stayed in this house for 25 years, hoping that she would come home. Now we can move on."

"We would like to know what funeral director you would like to use so we can have your daughter's remains taken directly there."

The woman stood up, went to the refrigerator, took a magnetic card from the door, and handed it to the Captain.

"This card has been there for many years, Captain. When you speak to them, please tell them we will be in touch about the funeral arrangements. We thank you very much for coming to tell us personally. Now would you both be good enough to leave my husband and I alone at this time?"

Both officers nodded and stood up. Both parents had tears on their cheeks as the officers exited the house.

Neither officer spoke as they climbed into the van and drove off.

"To the funeral home, Constable. Let's get it all over and done with. It never gets any easier telling families that a loved one is not coming home."

The two officers walked into the funeral home, where they were met by one of their staff. Before the Captain could speak, the funeral home person spoke.

"You have identified one of the deceased."

The Captain nodded.

"Yes. The remains will arrive tomorrow, and the parents will contact you regarding what funeral arrangements they want. However, I must caution that we do not want them cremated until we have a conviction of the perpetrator of the killing. Is that understood?"

"We understand, Captain. We will treat them with the respect that they deserve, and please arrest the evil people who have done this crime."

The two officers nodded and turned and left the funeral home.

"Back to the station, Constable. I need a strong coffee. I hate this part of being a police officer."

"I have to agree with you, Captain."

They entered the squad room and headed to the coffee machine. Two long flat whites with an extra shot of coffee.

The Captain headed for his office and the inevitable paperwork. He called over his shoulder, "Trip to the farm in one hour, Constable, if you please."

"Aye, aye, Captain."

The Captain shut his door and sat down. A tear rolled down his cheek. The sadness of the families of the one they just spoke to and the future ones when the DNA identified them depressed the Captain. He mopped up the tear and sipped his coffee. Well, at least the family now had closure. He finished his coffee and wondered what the Time Walker would make of it all.

The hour passed quickly, and the Captain and the Constable were back on the road heading to the farm.

The Captain hardly noticed the changes in the countryside as his thoughts were elsewhere.

There were only a few press people still hanging about as they turned into the farm.

The two officers climbed out of the van and walked through the trees to where the backhoe was just finishing excavating a grave site.

"Hello, everyone. How is it all going?"

"This is the last one, Captain. We have checked all around the farm, out to 250 metres from the farmhouse with the radar and walked all over the farm, and we cannot find any other evidence of more grave sites. I doubt that we will be able to identify some of the older graves going back 40 or 50 years, but we will do our best."

The captain called everyone to come closer. "You have all done a great job and a very difficult job under the circumstances, and all done with respect for the remains of the people who were buried here. I will ensure that the work you have done is recognised by the management in Sydney. Thank you from the bottom of my heart."

The sergeant was there, and the Captain indicated that he was to open the farm back up after the forensic people had departed. "I will speak to the remaining press as I leave and bring them up to date on where we are at this time. Bring all our people and equipment back to the station after the forensic people leave for Sydney. Your people have done some great work as well, sergeant. We have had a very busy few weeks, and now we have to tidy up all the loose ends and finish doing the paperwork. Please convey my heartfelt thanks to every member of the uniformed branch. Thank you."

"Constable, let's head back into town knowing that we will not be shot at anymore."

The van headed out to the gate and stopped at the farm gate. The Captain and the Constable, along with the uniformed gate guard, called the press over.

"Good day, everyone." The press gathered around.

"In a very short time, the forensic people will be finished, the backhoe will return to town, and the uniform branch will also leave these two farms devoid of any police presence. We have found the remains of seven souls buried here and one in the national park. We have identified the young lady from the national park by matching her DNA with her surviving parents. I will not give you her name out of respect to those parents who now have to go through the formality of burying their long-lost daughter. The forensic laboratory in Sydney is working hard to try and identify, using DNA and dental records, who the other persons are who were buried here.

Once the uniform branch leaves here, you are granted permission to film the farms as you find them. I would ask you to treat the subject with respect for the souls of the people whom we have exhumed from this farm."

"Are there any questions?"

"Captain, what progress are you making on finding out who the guilty persons are that did these crimes?"

"I am not at liberty to give out that information at this time; however, we are progressing and are further advanced than we were a week ago."

"What has happened to the people who were arrested from the farm across the road?"

"The only people who survived the shootout from the farm were chemists, and they are all in remand in Sydney. They will be tried for their crimes, and then any non-residents will be deported after sentences are served."

"Can you comment on the explosion that happened a couple of nights ago down in Canberra?"

"You will need to ask that question of the captain who is in charge of that district. Thank you all for your patience and good day."

The officers all turned and went back into the farm. The Captain and the Constable climbed into the van and drove off, leaving the press still waiting outside the two farms.

"Well, constable, I hope to never have anything like this farm ever again."

"Well, that makes two of us, Captain."

As the van drove off, the Captain's phone rang.

"Good afternoon, young fellow. You have been quiet ever since our foray down south."

"Captain, I have been doing a lot of research into the victims from this farm. When you get back to your office, you will find an attachment waiting for you with the names of the first three victims exhumed from the farm in the order in which they were discovered. I am working on the older graves found under the trees, and I will eventually give you a date they were buried; then, you need to go looking for people who were reported missing at that time.

Captain, I have spent a lot of money of late, and I would like the Commissioner to ensure that he puts in train the paperwork for the rewards that have been offered. I still have upgrades on my equipment to do.

Cheer up, Captain. We will wrap it all up soon. Good day."

The phone call ended.

"Well, constable, the young fellow has earned every penny that he is owed and more. I will take it up with the Commissioner when I get back to the office."

"Captain, we would not be where we are today without his help, and there would be a lot of blood on the streets as well."

"Constable, I would like a staff meeting tomorrow morning so we can work out where we are at on all these cases. Is 7:30 am too early, do you think?"

"No, Captain. I will notify everyone to be ready with their answers to your questions."

The Captain did some paperwork to end the day.

He strolled home through the twilight at the end of another autumn day.

The Captain arrived at the police station the next day at 7 am to find the squad room full of traffic branch and detectives all having a cup of coffee. There was a large box of blueberry muffins being consumed as well. The Captain joined in the conversations until 7:30 am when he called the squad room to order.

"All right, everyone, your attention please. I would like a heads-up on all the cases we have been involved in over the last few weeks. First, the crack house on the farm. Are there any outstanding issues?"

The chief detective replied. "Captain, the chemists have all been charged in Sydney with manufacturing drugs and explosives. There is little chance of them getting any bail as none of them had work permits, and they were involved in illegal activities. There are no other surviving persons from the crack house."

"Good, now the sleaze bag rapist. What's the status there?"

Chief detective spoke again.

"Captain, he has been refused bail due to the nature of his crimes and is being held in remand. We have tracked down all his victims, and all of them have sworn statements made against him. I doubt that he will see the sun outside of prison for twenty years based upon the assaults and rapes."

"The attempted shooting of the constable and myself is finished, as the shooter is deceased, as are the two shooters who tried to shoot me. That wraps up that crime scene."

"Now we come to the serial killers and the farm. The first victim from the national park has been identified, and her family is making arrangements for her remains to be buried. I have the names of the first three victims exhumed from the farm, now we need to ensure that through dental records or DNA, we are positive that they are who we think they are. Forensic will be finished doing the DNA tests soon. The older victims are yet to be tied to a time frame of when they were buried; then we can research the old records and find out who went missing at that time in our state history.

"Have we found out who has owned the farm over the last fifty years?"

"Captain, the farm is still owned by the old couple who have owned it for that time. The wife has passed away, and the husband resides in an old people's home, but he is senile and has dementia disease. The two twin sons are fighting over who should get the farm.

"Chief detective, have you found out who the snitch is in the Sydney police headquarters?"

"No, sir. All we were able to find out is that it was any number of phones used in the headquarters building."

"Very well. I would forget about that for the time being. We are also working on a strategy for the two sons at this time. Let's put that on hold for now. I don't want any discussion on matters related to the serial killings being made public, so everyone keep what you know to yourselves. There is a position vacant back of Woop, Woop for anyone blabbing about what they hear in this squad room. Thank you all for your time. I am very happy that we have been able to close off a lot of these cases."

Chapter 45

SERIAL KILLERS NAMED

The Captain topped up his mug of coffee and went to his office.

He had just sat down when his phone rang.

One glance was enough for the Captain to greet the Time Walker.

"Good morning, young fellow. How are you today?"

"Very well, Captain. Now, I promised you the identity of the killers of the young ladies that were buried at the farm.

I have sent you an attachment after I have edited out a lot of the violence. The video clearly shows the faces of the two brothers when they were twenty years younger than what they are today.

I would suggest that you arrest them in the most public place so a lot of people can witness their arrest. Keep them separate and play one off against the other. Disclose to the press that they have been arrested in relation to the young ladies' abduction and demise. If they manage to get bail, then I have another surprise for them.

I wish you the best of luck, Captain, and I will be watching closely what happens. Have a good day, Captain."

The phone went dead. The moment had come that the Captain had been dreading ever since the first time the Time Walker proved that he could do what he said he could.

The Captain booted up his laptop and then opened the file marked "evidence." The video showed the first young lady being dragged out of a van and being knocked to the ground. The violence escalated from there with beatings with the flat of the axe handles to violent rapes by the two brothers. The video then went on to the second victim, then the third victim, and finally the fourth victim, who was buried in the national park.

The Captain had seen some terrible sights during his police career, but nothing like he had just watched on his computer.

He shut the computer down and called for the Chief of Detectives and the Sergeant from the uniform branch.

They both arrived together.

"Gentlemen, I have just sent a photo to the printer. The photo is of two men in their fifties. Both well known about town in prominent positions in business and public affairs.

I want them arrested both at the same time and both of them in a very visible manner, with officers in uniform as well as detectives. I want them handcuffed and brought to the station, and you will park your cars outside the police station and bring them in through the TV cameras so we get the widest exposure to the general public. They are to be kept separate at all times. I will hold a press conference at that time. Are there any questions?

Please keep me informed when you arrive back here at the station. Thank you."

The Captain went and got a coffee and a shortbread biscuit, then returned to his office and sat down and waited.

An hour later, there was pandemonium outside the police station. The Captain stood up and walked to the front door of the station and looked out through the glass door at the melee outside the station. TV crews were shooting videos, and the press were yelling questions. Two men in handcuffs were being dragged through the crowd.

They were dragged by the police constables up the stairs and held upright at the top of the steps.

The Captain opened the door and went and stood on the front steps of the police station. He held his hand up for silence.

"Good morning, all. What you are seeing at this time are the two suspects whom we believe have been responsible for the abduction and killings of four of the victims that we have exhumed from 'Hill Top Farm.'

We have other evidence that ties them to the crimes, and as time goes on, this will be made known to the press. Now we have arrested them, and we will compare fingerprints and DNA with what we have been able to gather from the farm.

Thank you for your patience in this matter."

The Captain indicated to the arresting officers to take the suspects away. The suspects were yelling, "This is bullshit. I had nothing to do with those killings. I want a lawyer."

The Captain shut the police station door and said in a loud voice, "Get these animals out of my sight. Get them into a cell but keep them separate."

He walked back to the squad room and turned on the television to see the brothers being taken from the police cars into the police station.

By now, everyone in the town would be ringing their family and friends and telling them to turn on the TV and see what was happening. People would be putting two and two together and saying, "Well, they have always had the farm, so who else could have gone there and buried the bodies?"

"Sarge."

"Yes, Captain."

"High visible presence around the streets for the next 24 hours. These arrests are going to spark a lot of arguments and fights when people get a few beers inside them."

"Chief Detective, my office, please."

The Chief Detective was there in moments.

"Yes, sir."

"Get our best interrogators onto these animals as soon as possible. Play one off against the other; see if one of them will turn crown witness for a lesser sentence. They will both see the rest of their days out inside a maximum-security prison."

"Captain, how do you know they are the guilty persons?"

"Chief Detective, have a look at this video."

The Captain clicked on the video, and the Chief Detective started watching. He turned away after a couple of minutes. The Captain turned the computer around and shut it down.

"They were the only ones who had access to the farm to do their foul deeds and to have the time to bury the evidence. Now, if we can't break them, we will let them go. Can you imagine their life in this town from now on if we are forced to release them by our legal system? I am sure parts of this video will crop up from time to time whenever they are out from their homes.

I imagine they won't have many friends anymore."

The Chief Detective stood up. "We will do our best to get a confession, Captain."

Four hours later, the Chief Detective returned and knocked on the Captain's door.

"Come in. Ah, Chief Detective. What news?"

"They both keep saying the same thing, Captain. 'I am innocent and want a lawyer.'"

"Right. Captain, ensure they contact their lawyer, and when he arrives, please bring him directly to myself.

Have I.T. set up a computer screen in one of the interrogation rooms that I can plug my laptop into. When we bring them up from the cells, make sure they are in ankle bracelets and handcuffs, and lock them to the desk before I bring in the lawyer. I want all the chairs facing the screen, and I also want a plastic bucket in the room next to the table.

Here is a search warrant for their offices and residences. I am very interested in their passports, as I have a sneaking suspicion that they go to Singapore every year en route to the poorer countries of Asia, where they can continue their dirty activities with the help of the criminal elements of that country. Also, look out for trophies, as like the sleazy rapist, a lot of them keep trophies of their killings, so search everywhere."

"On our way, Captain."

The Captain sat back in his chair and thought about what was going to happen when the solicitor arrived. He would be coming from Sydney for sure, as none of the local solicitors had any criminal experience other than for break-and-enter crimes, speeding, DUI, and fighting in the hotels.

It was mid-afternoon when the Chief Detective brought a well-dressed gentleman into the Captain's office. The Captain stood up and introduced himself.

"Good afternoon, Captain Wilson. How do you do?"

The lawyer looked down his nose at the Captain. "Paul Winthrop of Winthrop and Winthrop and Partners. I am here to see my clients, Robert and Andrew Peters, who I believe you have in the cells here in your country station."

"Please take a seat, Paul, and I will arrange for them to be brought up from the cells to an interview room."

"You see that crowd gathering outside the police station, Paul?"

"Yes, I did. What is all that about?"

"They are family and friends of the four young ladies whose remains we have exhumed from the Peters farm. If they get their hands on the Bobbsies twins, they will lynch them."

"But surely you can tell them to go home? After all, you are the police."

"Mate, feelings are running very high in the town at the moment. I have the riot squad arriving at any time from Sydney, but they will only be ten men, plus my uniform branch. We would not have a hope in hell of stopping them from dragging your clients out of the police station."

"Captain, they are innocent until proven guilty."

"Well, Paul, we are going to go down to the interview room and watch a short video. Then you can make up your own mind what you recommend to your clients. Follow me."

The Captain stood up and led the way through the station, down the stairs to the interview room. He was carrying his laptop and cable. The two alleged killers were shackled to the table.

"Take a seat, Paul." The laptop was set on the table and plugged in.

"Captain, I need to speak to my clients alone, if you don't mind."

"Not a problem, Paul, but first, all of you watch this video."

The solicitor and the twin accused seemed puzzled as the screen lit up, showing the twins dragging one of the girls out of a van and starting to beat her with the flats of the axe handles. The video progressed from there to more horrific violence, with the twins raping the girls and more beatings until she was dead. They then dropped her in the bottom of the future rubbish pit.

The Captain looked at the solicitor. He had gone white and had his eyes closed.

"Not very nice, was it, Mr. Paul from Winthrop and Winthrop? Now that video was sent to me by a genius, and I believe it is already standing by in every hotel in this town, ready to be shown on their television screens. You can apply to the court for bail; however, I have doubts that you will get bail. How about it, boys? Do you want bail so you can go out into the town, and wherever you go, this video will show up on a television screen, and you will be lucky to live the week out? Another option is you can stay safe and sound in remand and wait for trial.

You will never be able to plead innocent and have anyone believe you, not with the evidence we have against you. You can, of course, confess and sign a confession and have it witnessed by your solicitor, and throw yourself on the mercy of the court.

I will leave you all now to discuss your future, or lack thereof."

Knock on the door when you want to leave, Mr. Paul.

The Captain took his computer and left the room.

The two twins were thunderstruck and never uttered a word.

The solicitor did not even want to look at the two killers.

The Captain went back to his office and put on the kettle. When his kettle boiled, he made himself a nice Earl Grey cup of tea and took a couple of shortbread biscuits and settled down to wait.

Forty minutes later, there was a knock at the Captain's door.

"Come in. Ah, Mr. Paul from Winthrop and Winthrop. How did your talk to the twins go?

Are they going for bail so they can go out and face the people who want to hang them, or are they going to throw themselves on the mercy of the court?"

"Captain, my apologies for my attitude when I first arrived here. When I saw that video, I had to close my eyes as I could not believe that anyone could do what they had done to another human being just for enjoyment. They have both signed confessions, witnessed by myself and one of your civilian workers from your office. They will not be able to rebut the confessions at a later time. I will not be representing them in court having seen that video, which I am not sure is real or not, but the twins believed what they were seeing."

"Paul, have a cup of Earl Grey tea and sit quietly for a minute."

The Captain passed a cup of tea across to the lawyer, which was gratefully received. "Sugar and milk to your taste from the sideboard there.

"The video is real, Paul. I cannot tell you how we came to be in possession of it, but in the future, Artificial Intelligence will revolutionize police work and catch a lot more criminals. Let's just leave it at that. Now we need to ensure that we can get you away from here in one piece. We will put you inside a police vehicle and take you back to your vehicle. I will hold a news conference at the same time, which will keep everybody occupied."

"Sarge."

"Yes, Captain."

"Take Mister Paul back to his vehicle in a police vehicle, just like he is a police plainclothes person, so these people out the front don't give him any grief."

They both stood up, and the lawyer put out his hand and shook the Captain's hand.

"Thank you, Captain. I hope to meet you again sometime under better circumstances."

The Captain nodded.

"Constable, Chief Detective, a minute please."

Both of them appeared like magic.

"Right, call the riot squad in from their vehicles and have them form a line between the station and the press out the front. When they are all in position, I will address all the people out front, so I might need a megaphone to be able to talk over the noise. Give me a call when they are in position. I don't expect any problems, but you never know what a few hotheads can do."

Everyone vacated the office and disappeared to organize things for the Captain's press conference outside the station.

The Captain stood up and added his bulletproof vest and shoulder holster, complete with his Glock. His suit coat went over the top.

He took his phone and rang the commissioner.

Only one ring this time. The commissioner was getting jittery with calls from the Captain.

"Captain, what can I do for you?"

"Commissioner, we have signed confessions from the evil twins, witnessed by their solicitor, so they can go to the remand centre tonight about 2 a.m. when it is cold, and there will not be many people about. I have just called the riot squad to form a line between the press and the station, and I will go out in a few minutes and address the press and the crowd of locals who are very agitated about finding out that their Mayor and one of their distinguished citizens are serial killers."

"Captain, you be very careful there as it does not take much to start a riot. If anything happens, lock yourselves in the police station and let me know immediately, and I will get officers from the surrounding towns across to you all within 30 minutes."

"Thanks, Commissioner. I will call you later."

A knock at the door signalled that all was ready for the Captain.

The Captain stood and walked out through the squad room, taking the megaphone from the desk as he passed. Every officer in the station was standing ready to go out front if required.

The Captain opened the front door, and the noise from 500 people all shouting at once was deafening.

The Captain stood behind his riot police, who had blocked off access to the station steps.

The Captain lifted the megaphone and called out for silence.

"If you are not silent, you will not hear what I am going to say."

The press were filming away and talking into their microphones.

"Quiet, please."

Slowly the noise died down.

"I want to take this opportunity to bring the press and the people of this community up to date on what has happened over the last couple of weeks. We have exhumed the remains of a young lady who went missing from this town twenty-five years ago when I was a young constable just stationed here. That event nearly tore this town apart with suspicion and conspiracy theories. I know that the parents of that young lady will want to inter her with the respect and dignity that she deserves, and this town owes her that same respect.

We have also exhumed, on the 'Hill Top' farm, the remains of seven more persons.

You all know we have arrested the Mayor and his brother in relation to four of those bodies.

This morning both of those people have signed confessions related to the abduction, assault, and murders of those people."

The remaining four graves that were found on the farm related to crimes committed over fifty years ago. Those people were abducted and murdered by the parents of the two men being held in custody. Their mother has been dead for some seven years, and their father is in an old persons' home suffering from senility and dementia. He will soon be judged by a higher authority than the laws of this state. The crimes that have been committed by these men are abhorrent, and they will end up spending the rest of their lives in prison. I now want the press and the people of this town to quietly disperse and allow the police to continue their work to find out the identities of the seven people who, at this time, are unknown, as we are still waiting on DNA testing and identification by the forensic people.

We are very close to having those names and knowing where they came from.

Thank you for your time."

The captain dropped the megaphone to his side and waited.

The crowd just stood there, as if waiting for something else to happen. Then a few people at the sides of the crowd slowly walked away, and then the whole lot turned and walked away, all talking to each other.

Within minutes, only the press was still there.

"Are there any questions that you would like to ask me in a civilized manner?"

"Captain, do you expect to find any further evidence of serial killings in the district?"

"I believe, and the federal police are investigating, the overseas trips these brothers took to developing countries and what they did while they were there. We have found no evidence of any further serial killings in this district.

Ladies and gentlemen of the press, this is the last time I will speak to you regarding events that have happened here over the last few weeks. These include the crack drug house, the serial killings, and the attempts on my life by various people. All future press conferences will be held in Sydney by the police commissioner. Good day."

The Captain turned and walked back into the police station.

The whole station breathed a sigh of relief, then a lot of people started talking at once.

The Captain walked through the press of officers and into his office and sat down.

He could feel the tension draining out of his body.

The Captain's phone rang.

"Hello, Commissioner."

"Well, Captain, thanks for handballing the press conference over to me. However, you and your people have done a great job over the last few weeks. I will be in touch soon about a special assignment coming up for yourself. Good day."

The phone went dead.

The phone rang.

"Hello, young fellow. Don't you think it is about time I had a name to call you instead of the disrespectful term 'young fellow'?"

"Captain, I am quite happy with 'young fellow.' I know you are not disrespectful. Now, have a look at your emails and you will see the names of the three other people murdered by the evil twins. I'm sure that I gave these to you at an earlier time, plus the dates that the other four persons were buried by their evil parents.

If you go back through the old police records, you will be able to find out the names of people who disappeared at that time around the state."

"Please have the commissioner make arrangements to pay me any rewards due, though the rewards offered fifty years ago will only buy me a McDonald's hamburger and a couple of hash browns today.

Captain, I think you deserve a good holiday and not just two days down the coast.

I will be talking to the commissioner regarding a promotion for Constable Wilkens. She deserves that for the hours and effort she has put in on the cases we have been working on.

Talk later, Captain."

The phone went dead.

The Captain felt very weary, and the thought of some time off was appealing.

The commissioner had other ideas.

www.ingramcontent.com/pod-product-compliance
Lightning Source LLC
Chambersburg PA
CBHW070109120726
47909CB00002B/549